THE DAY MOM FINALLY SNAP-PED

LIBRARIAN REVIEWER

Laurie K. Holland

Media Specialist (National Board Certified), Edina, MN

MA in Elementary Education, Minnesota State University, Mankato, MN

READING CONSULTANT

Elizabeth Stedem

Educator/Consultant, Colorado Springs, CO

MA in Elementary Education, University of Denver, CO

Graphic Sparks are published by Stone Arch Books,
151 Good Counsel Drive, P.O. Box 669,
Mankato, Minnesota 56002.
www.stonearchbooks.com

Library of Congress Cataloging-in-Publication Data
Temple, Bob.
The Day Mom Finally Snapped / by Bob Temple; illustrated by Steve Harpster.
p. cm. — (Graphic Sparks)
ISBN-13: 978-1-59889-038-9 (hardcover)
ISBN-10: 1-59889-038-7 (hardcover)
ISBN-13: 978-1-59889-170-6 (hardcover)
ISBN-10: 1-59889-170-7 (hardcover)
1. Graphic novels. I. Harpster, Steve. II. Title. III. Series.
PN6727.T2945D39 2006
741.5—dc22 2005026685

Summary: She's the best mom in the world! She never yells or gets mad. She only asks questions like, "Are you trying to drive me crazy?!" Willy, Tom, and Grace want to surprise Mom by painting their rooms. What could possibly go wrong? And why is there smoke coming from Mom's ears?

Art Director: Heather Kindseth
Production Manager: Sharon Reid
Production/Design: James Liebman, Mie Tsuchida
Production Assistance: Bob Horvath, Eric Murray

1 2 3 4 5 6 11 10 09 08 07 06

Printed in the United States of America.

THE DAY MOM FINALLY SNAP~PED

BY BOB TEMPLE

ILLUSTRATED BY STEVE HARPSTER

STONE ARCH BOOKS
MINNEAPOLIS   SAN DIEGO

CAST OF CHARACTERS

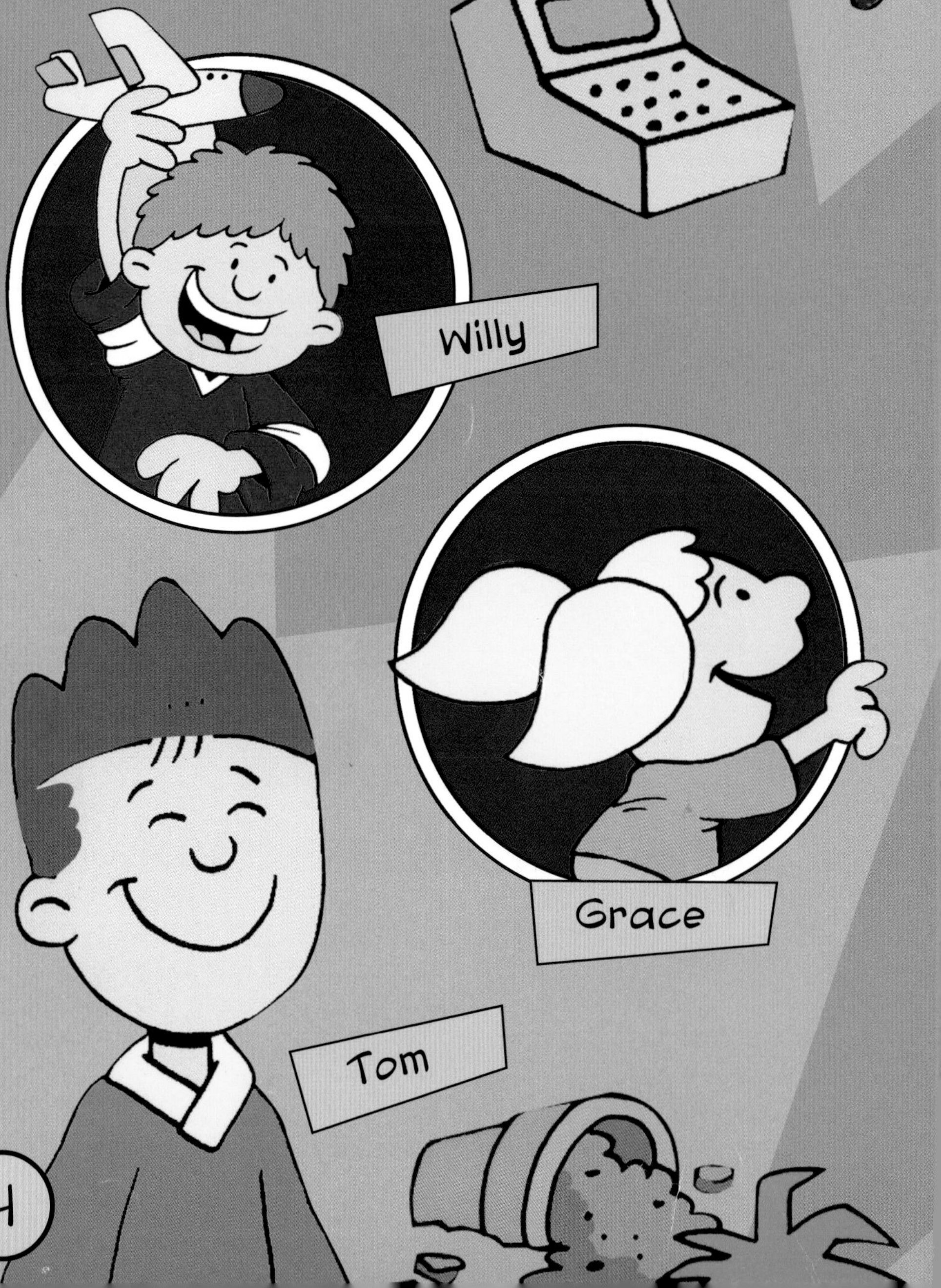
Willy
Grace
Tom

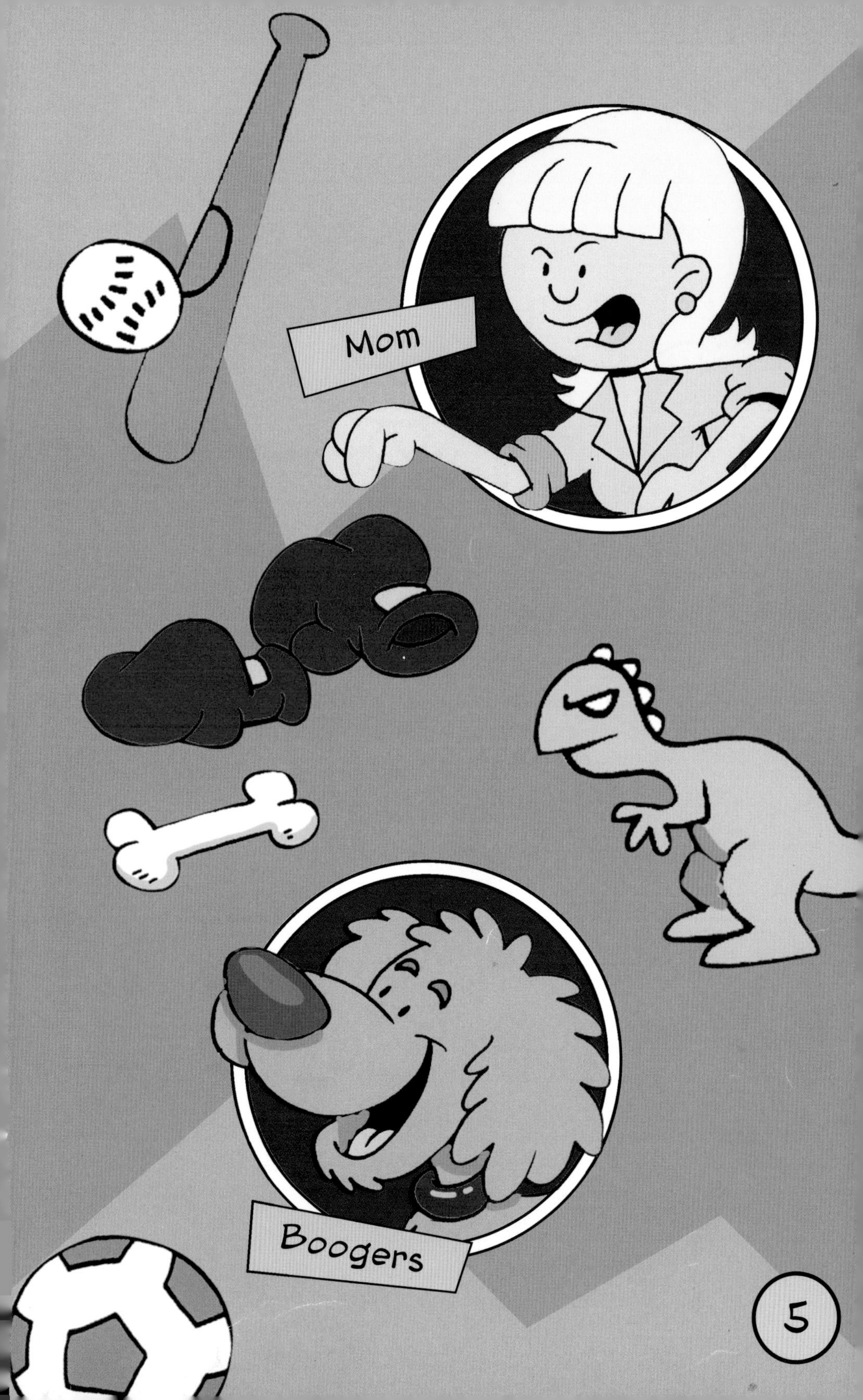
Mom
Boogers

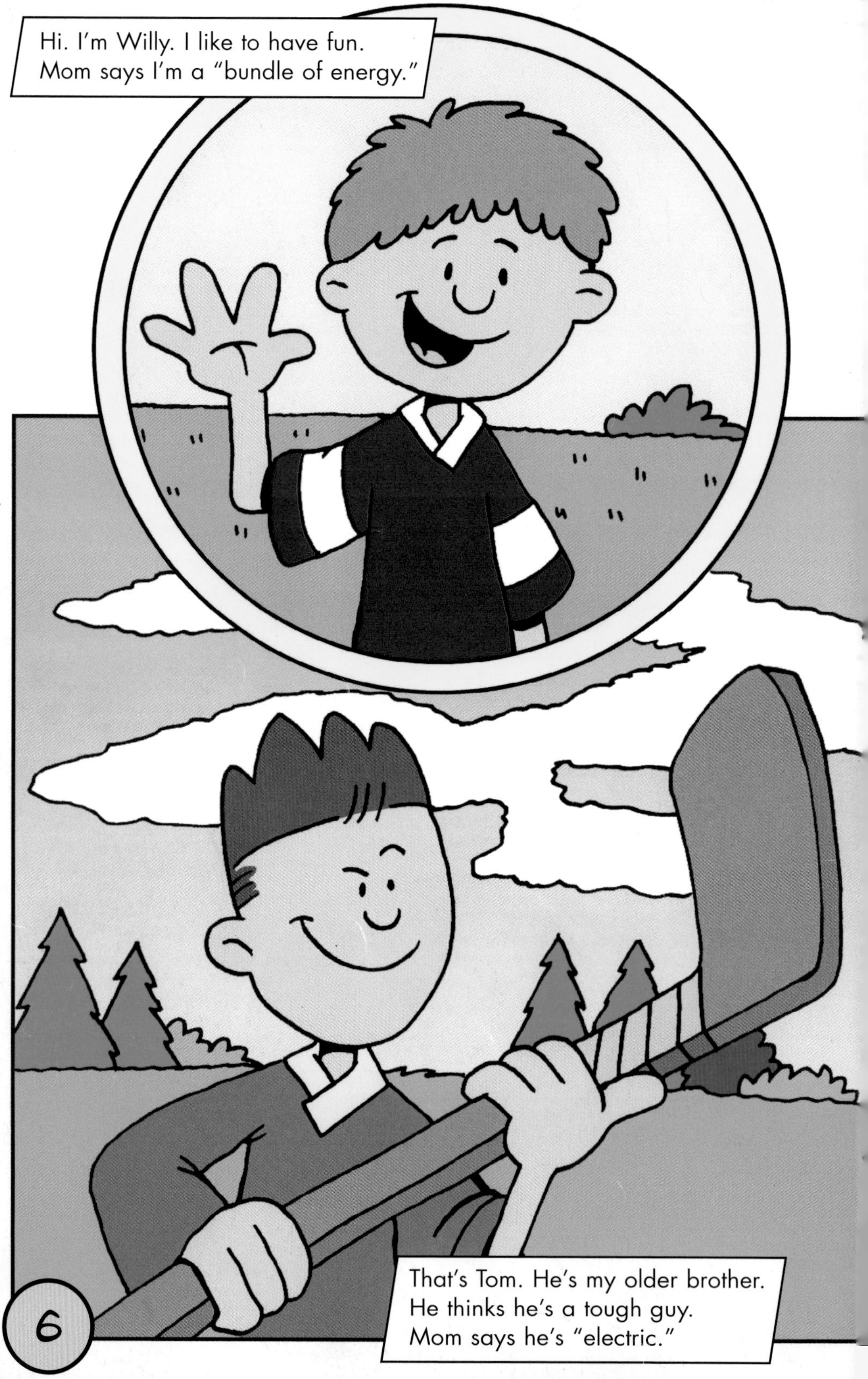
Hi. I'm Willy. I like to have fun.
Mom says I'm a "bundle of energy."
That's Tom. He's my older brother.
He thinks he's a tough guy.
Mom says he's "electric."

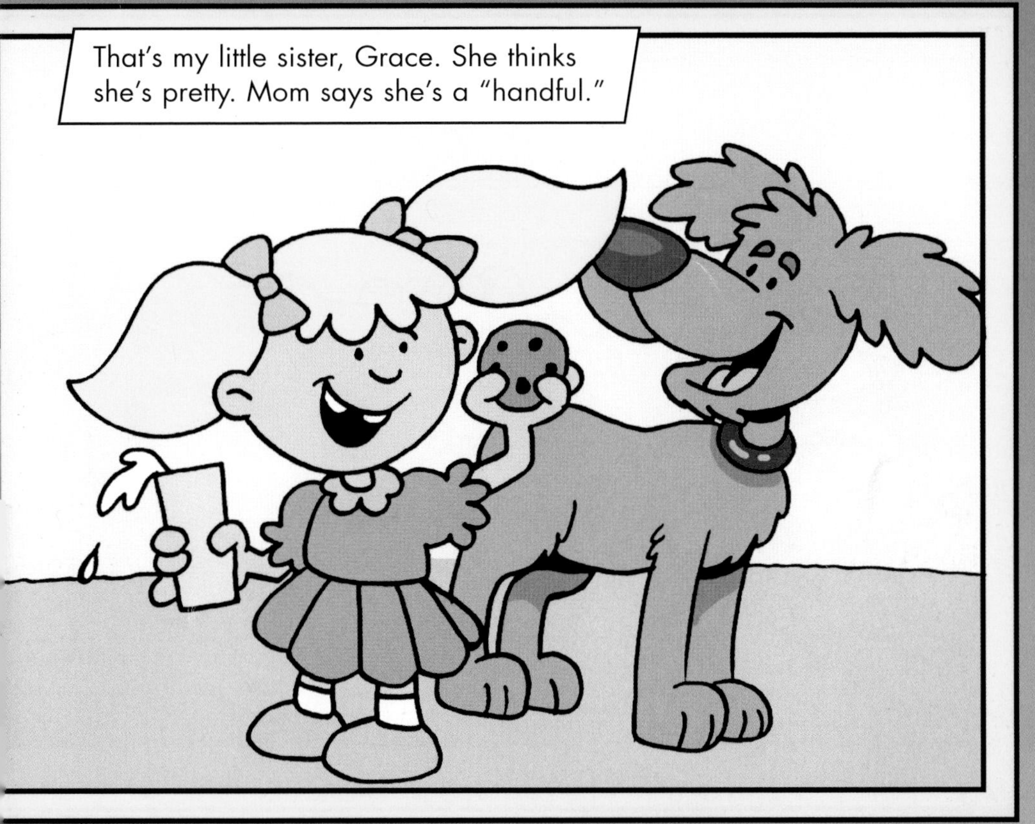
That's my little sister, Grace. She thinks she's pretty. Mom says she's a "handful."

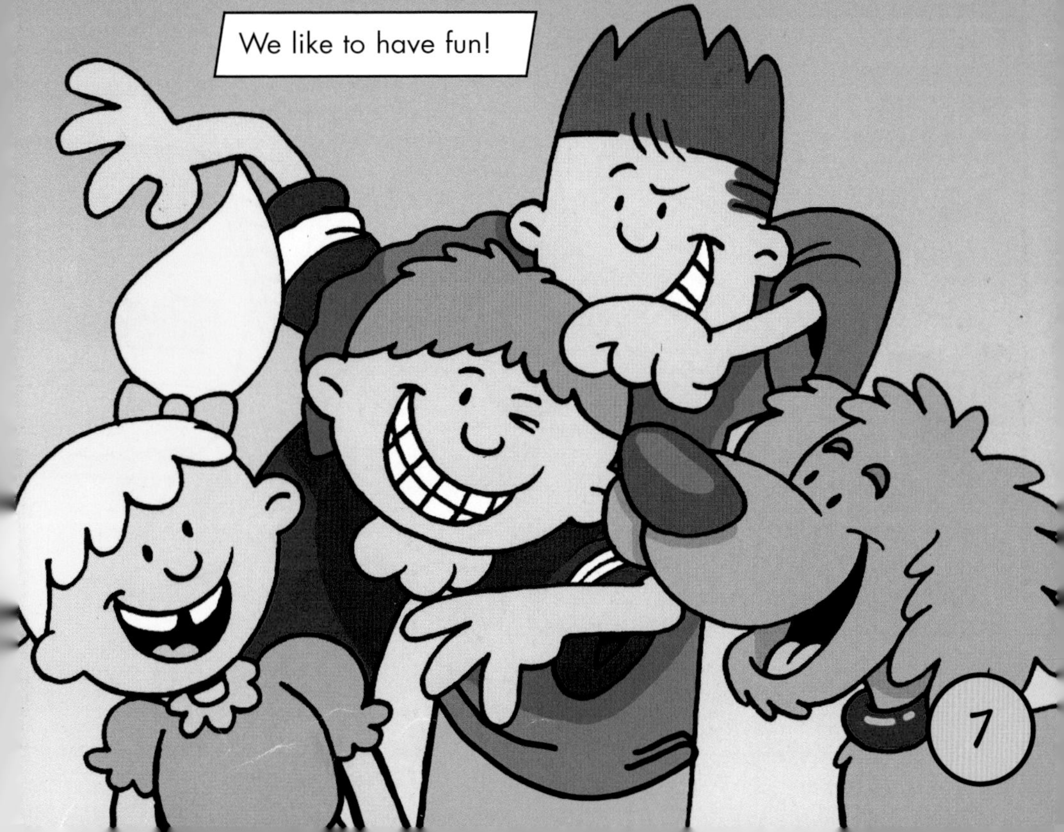
We like to have fun!

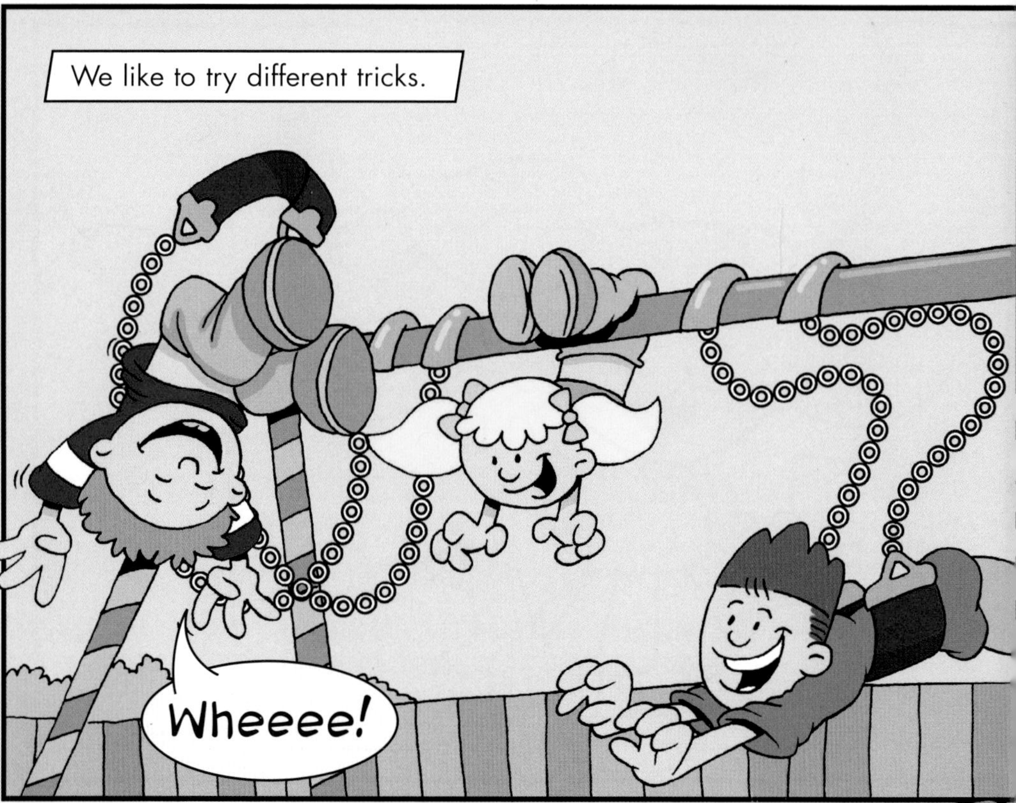
We like to try different tricks.
Wheeeee!

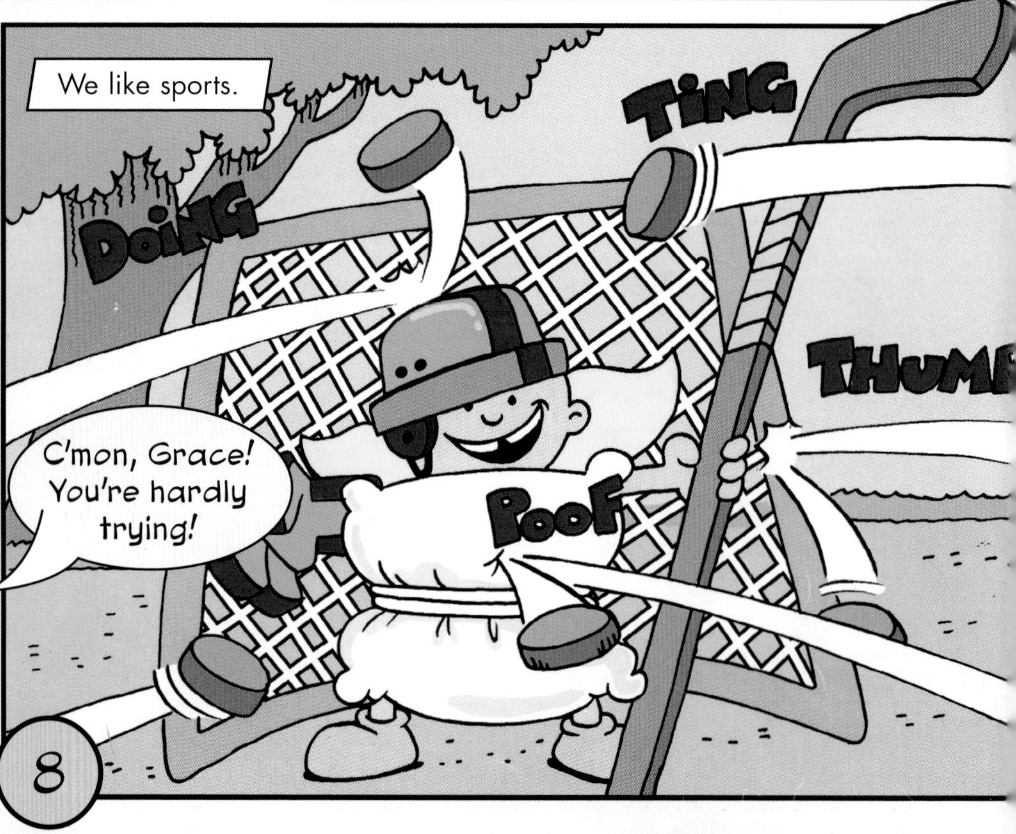
We like sports.
TING
DOING
C'mon, Grace! You're hardly trying!
POOF

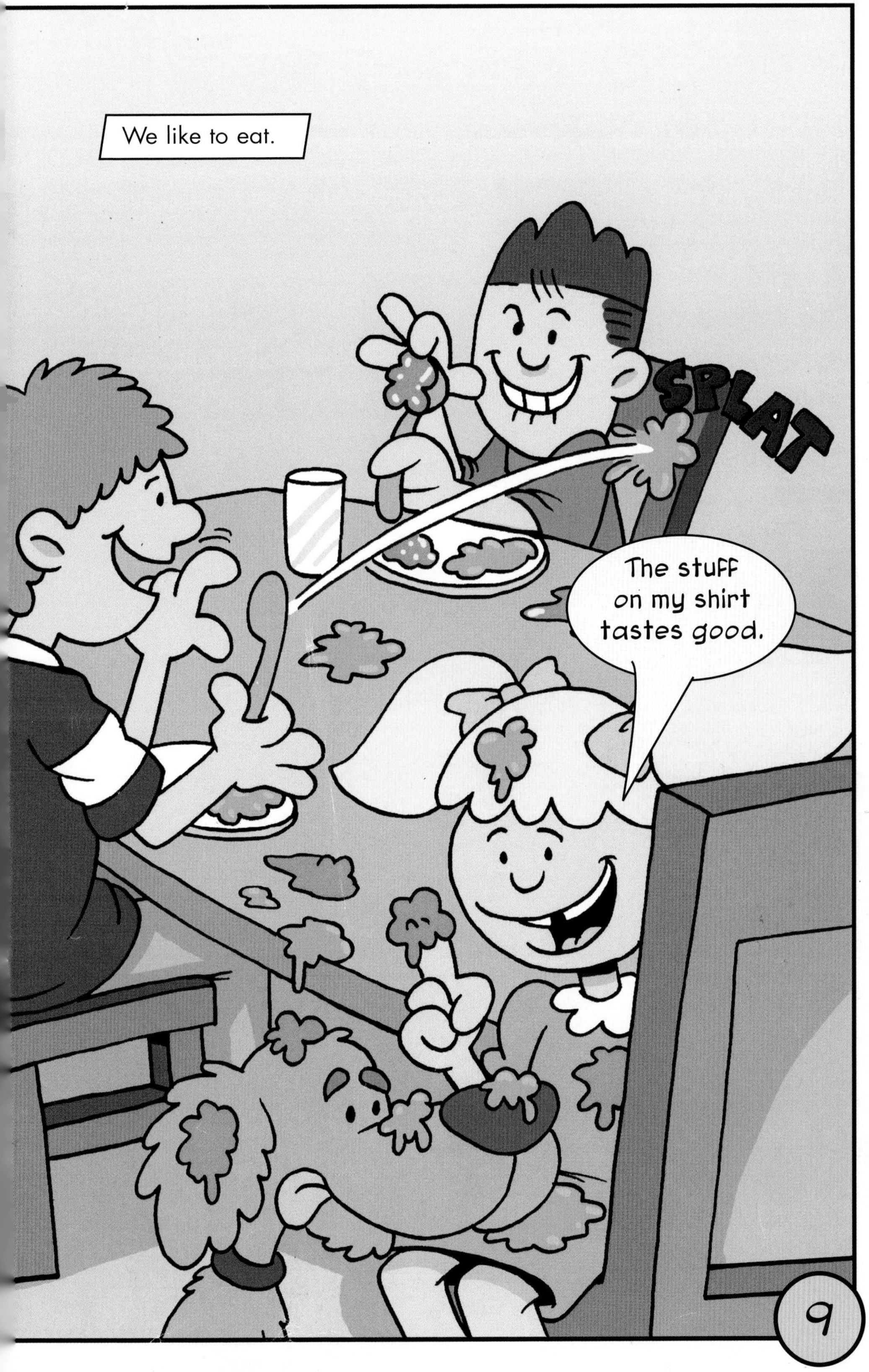
We like to eat.
SPLAT
The stuff on my shirt tastes good.

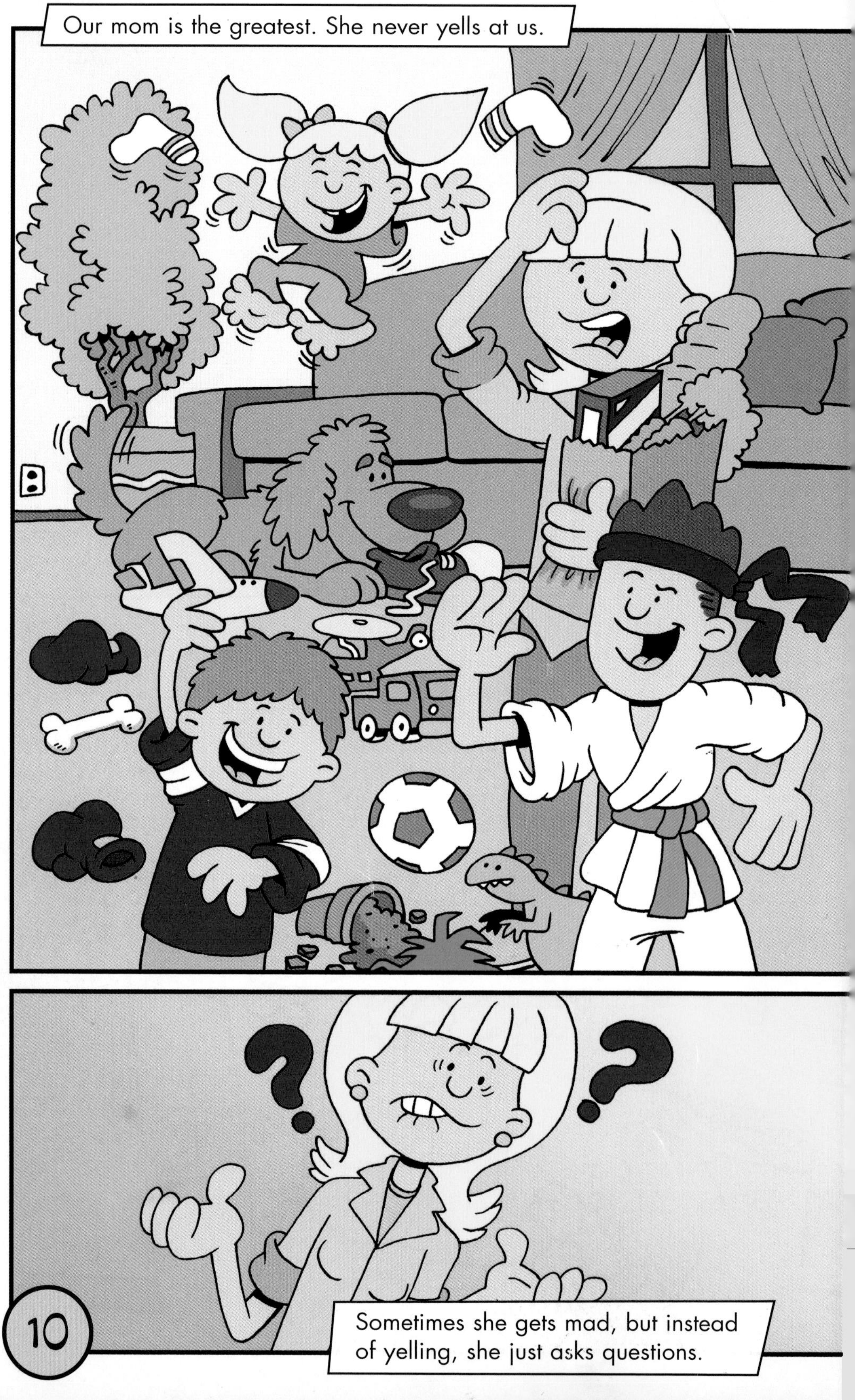
Our mom is the greatest. She never yells at us.
Sometimes she gets mad, but instead of yelling, she just asks questions.

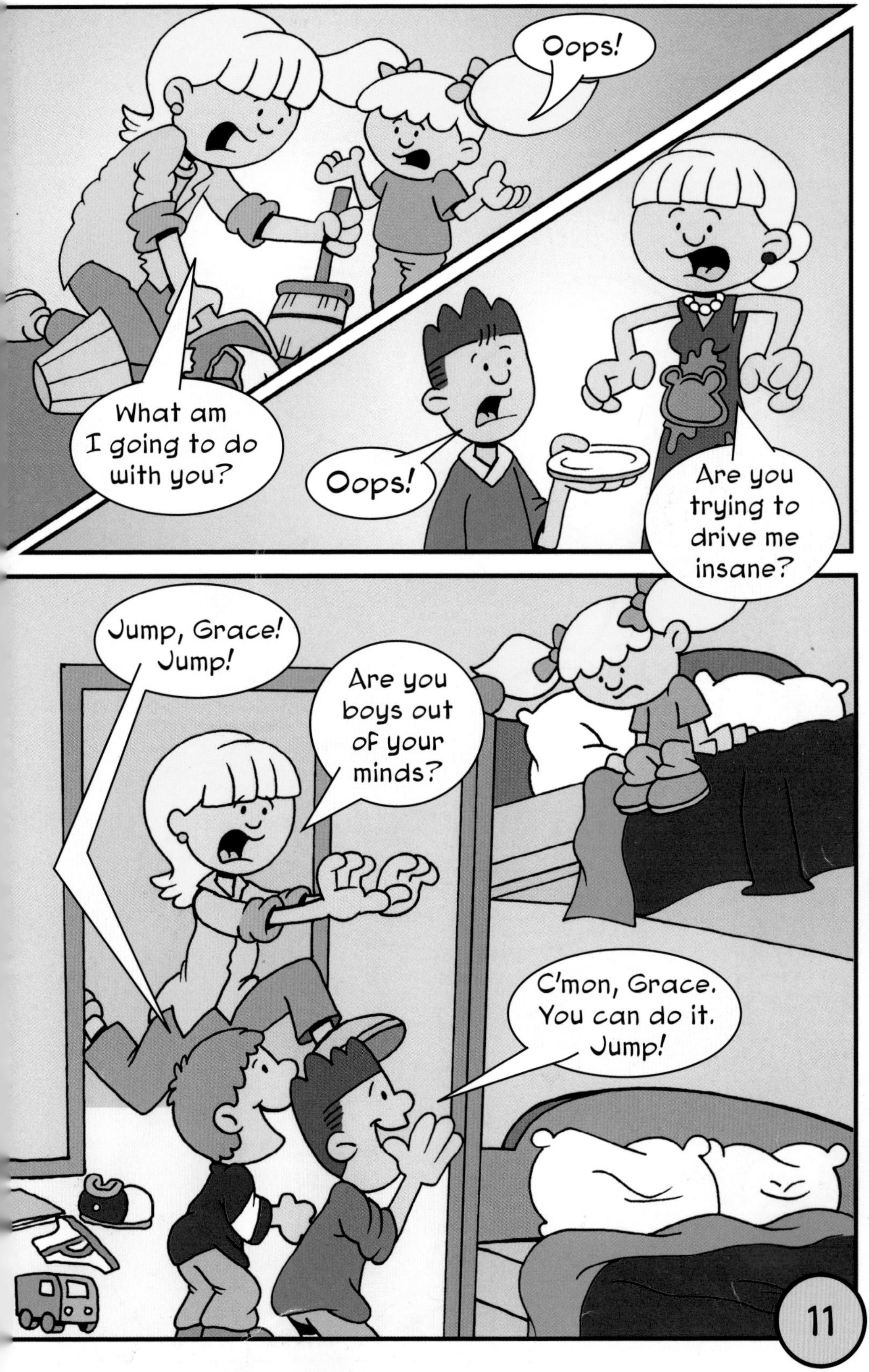
Oops!
What am I going to do with you?
Oops!
Are you trying to drive me insane?
Jump, Grace! Jump!
Are you boys out of your minds?
C'mon, Grace. You can do it. Jump!

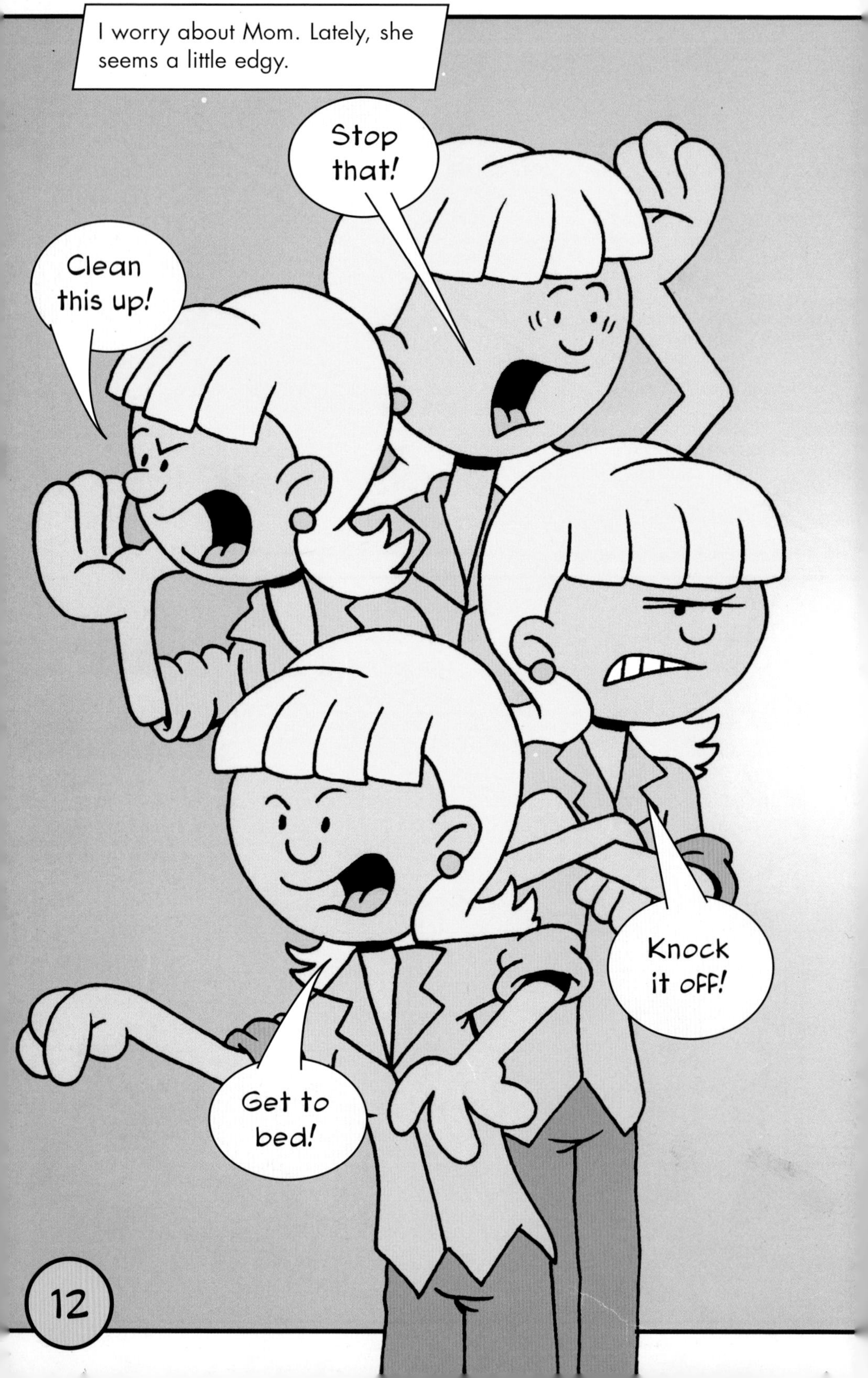
I worry about Mom. Lately, she seems a little edgy.
Stop that!
Clean this up!
Knock it off!
Get to bed!

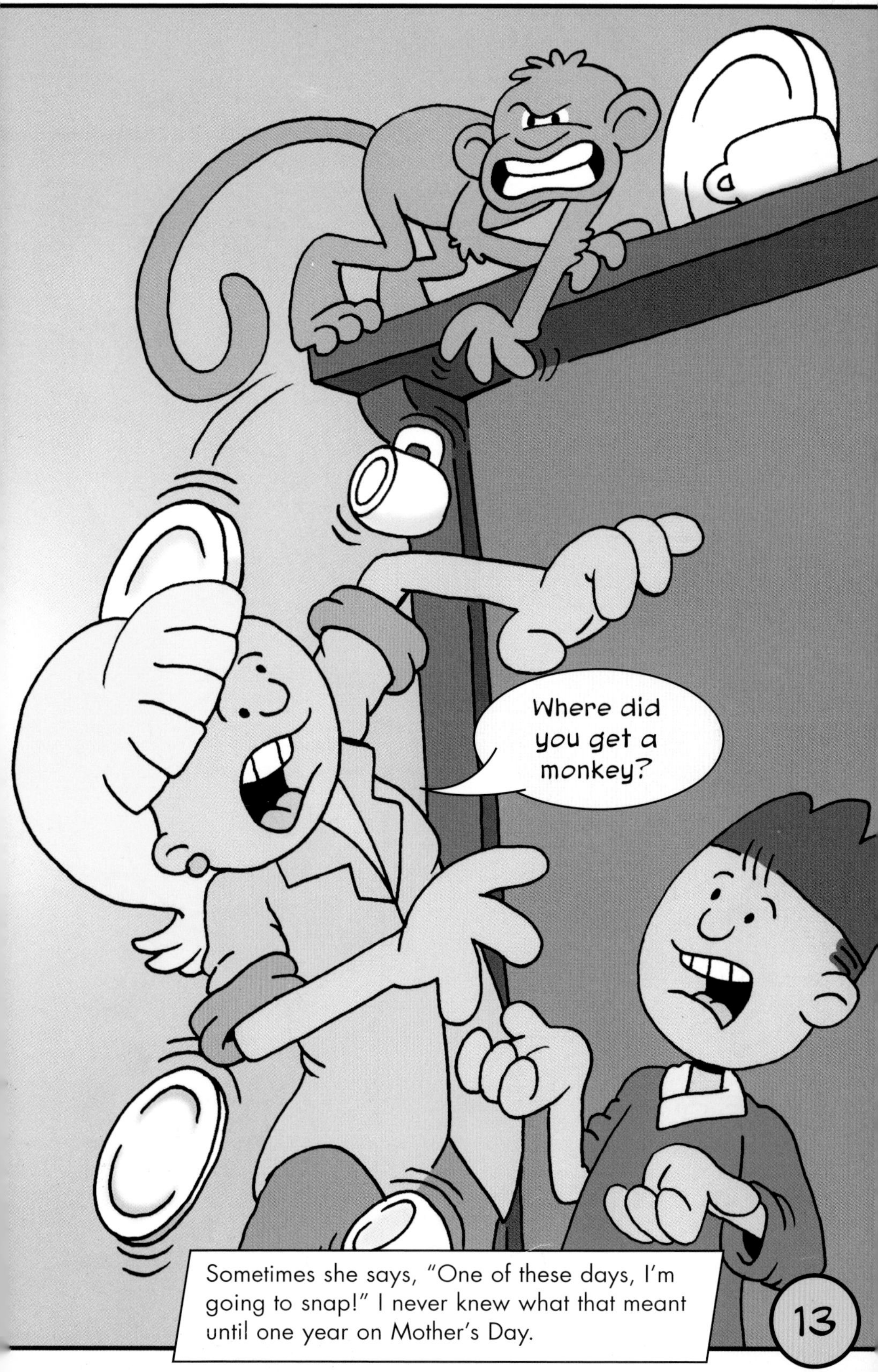
Where did you get a monkey?

Sometimes she says, "One of these days, I'm going to snap!" I never knew what that meant until one year on Mother's Day.

That year, we decided to treat Mom to a special day. It all started when we woke up very early. Really, we were just trying to be nice.
Hey, Willy, do you like our room?
4:30
Not really. I'm not a baby anymore.

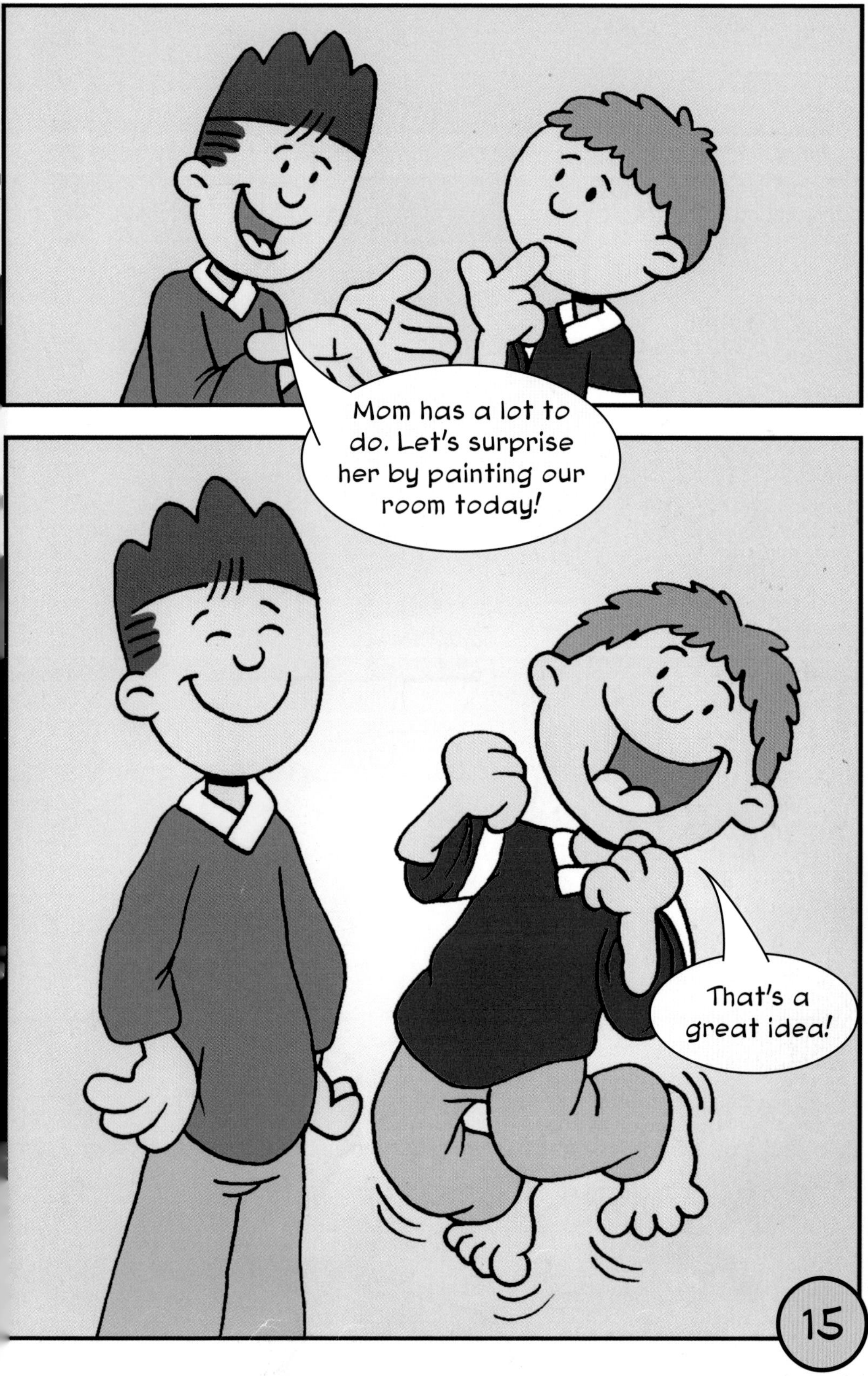
Mom has a lot to do. Let's surprise her by painting our room today!
That's a great idea!

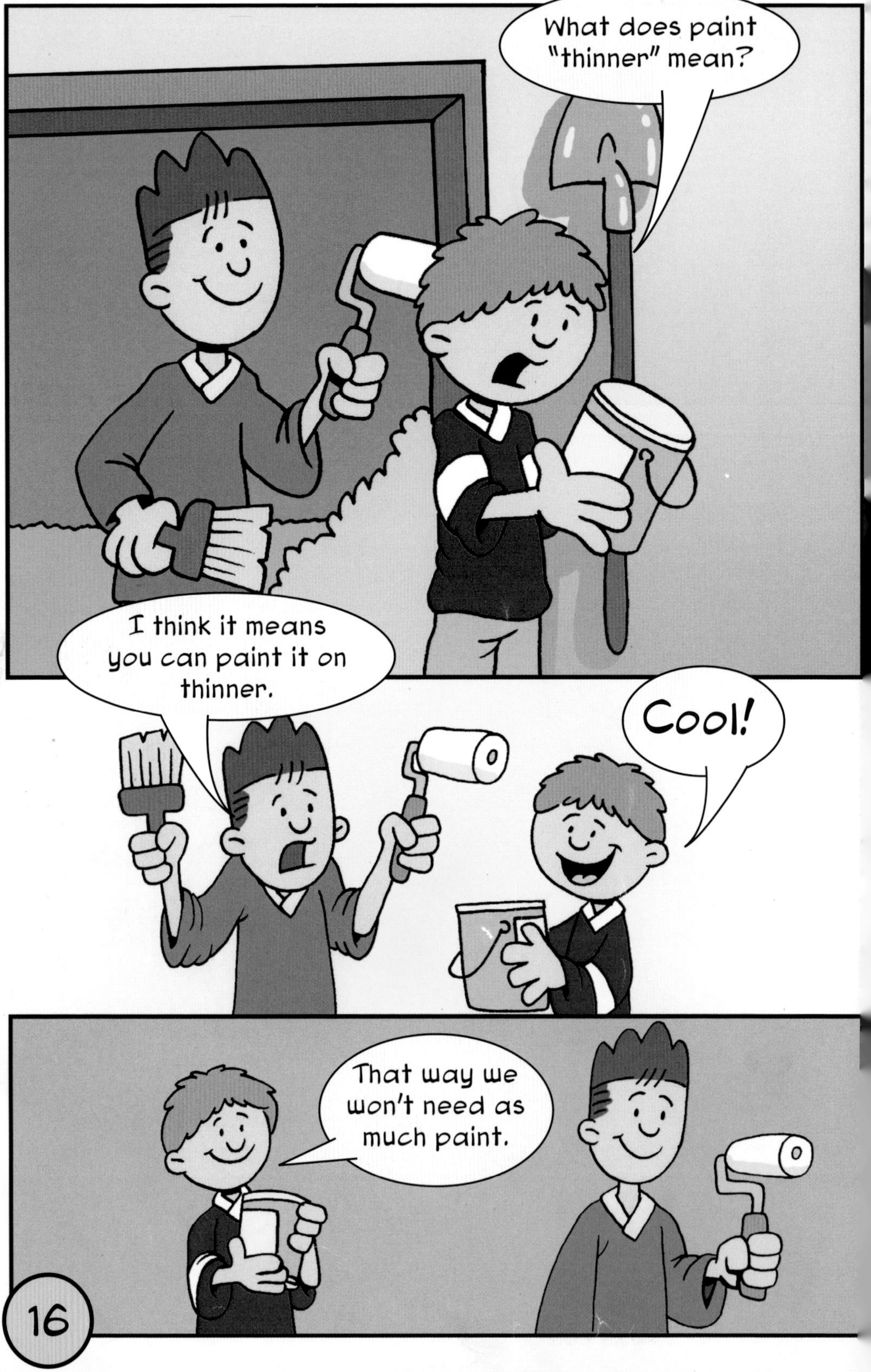
What does paint "thinner" mean?
I think it means you can paint it on thinner.
Cool!
That way we won't need as much paint.

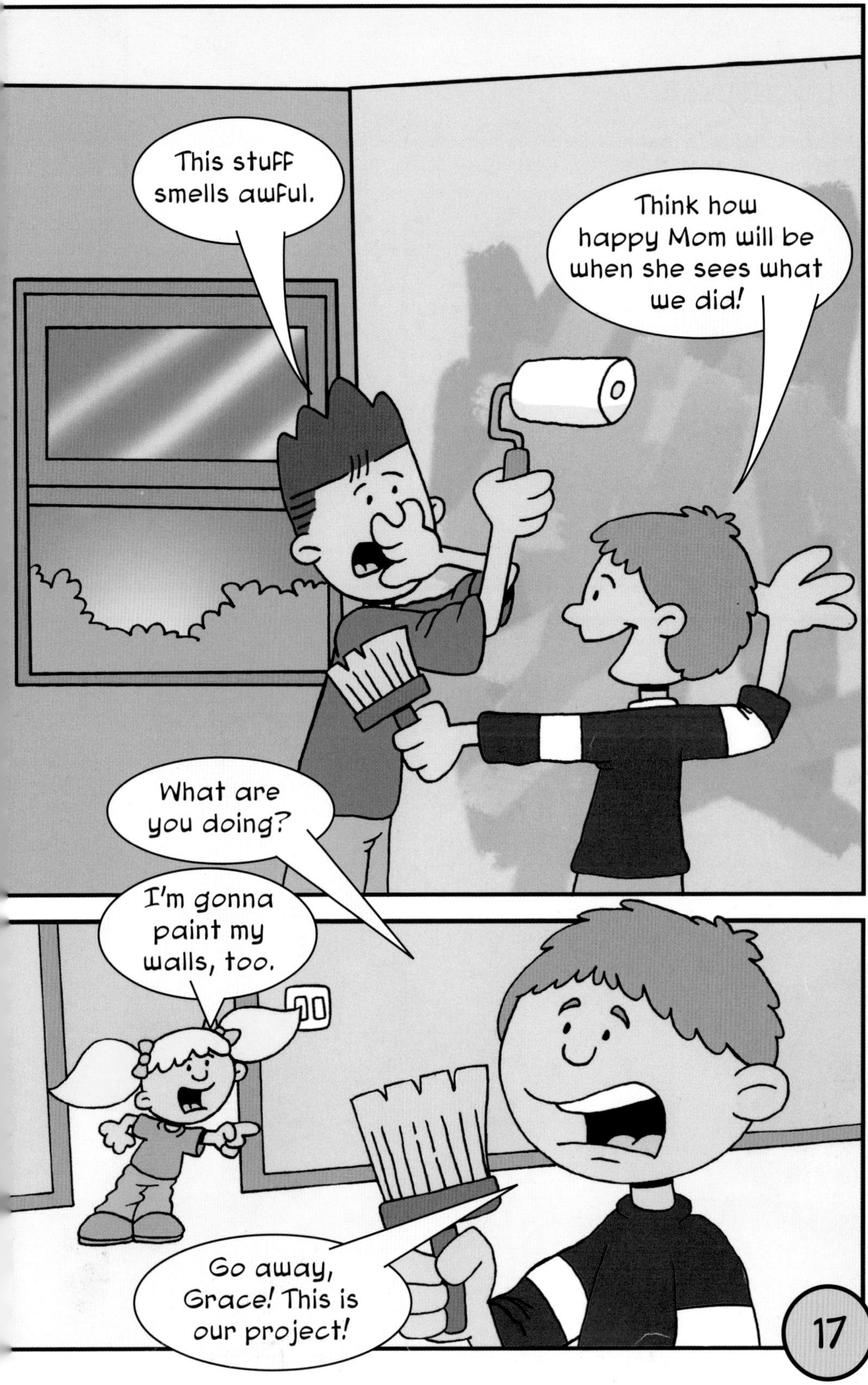
This stuff smells awful.
Think how happy Mom will be when she sees what we did!
What are you doing?
I'm gonna paint my walls, too.
Go away, Grace! This is our project!

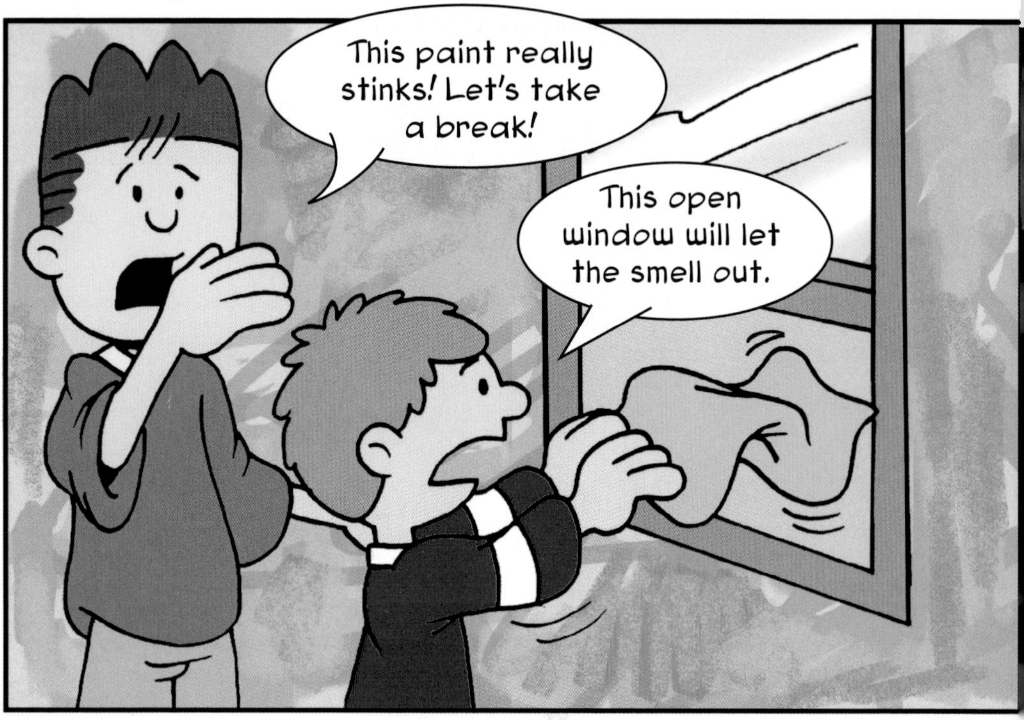
This paint really stinks! Let's take a break!
This open window will let the smell out.

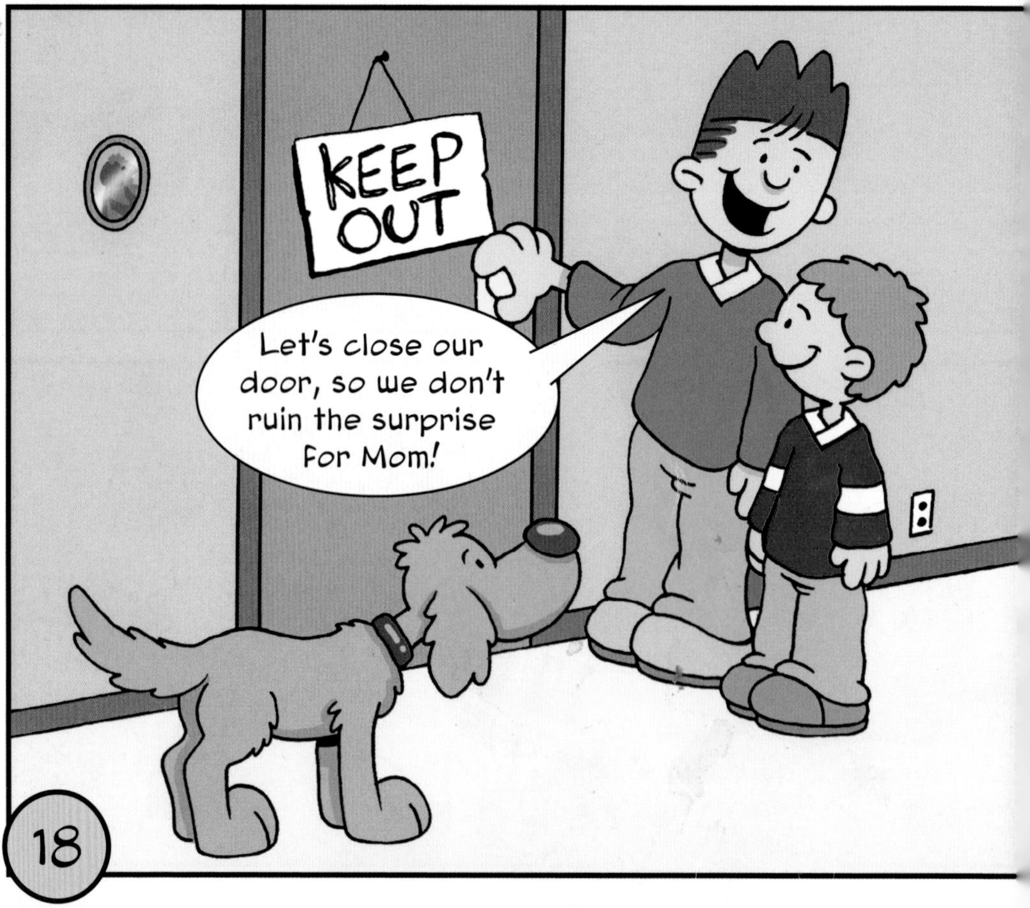
KEEP OUT
Let's close our door, so we don't ruin the surprise for Mom!

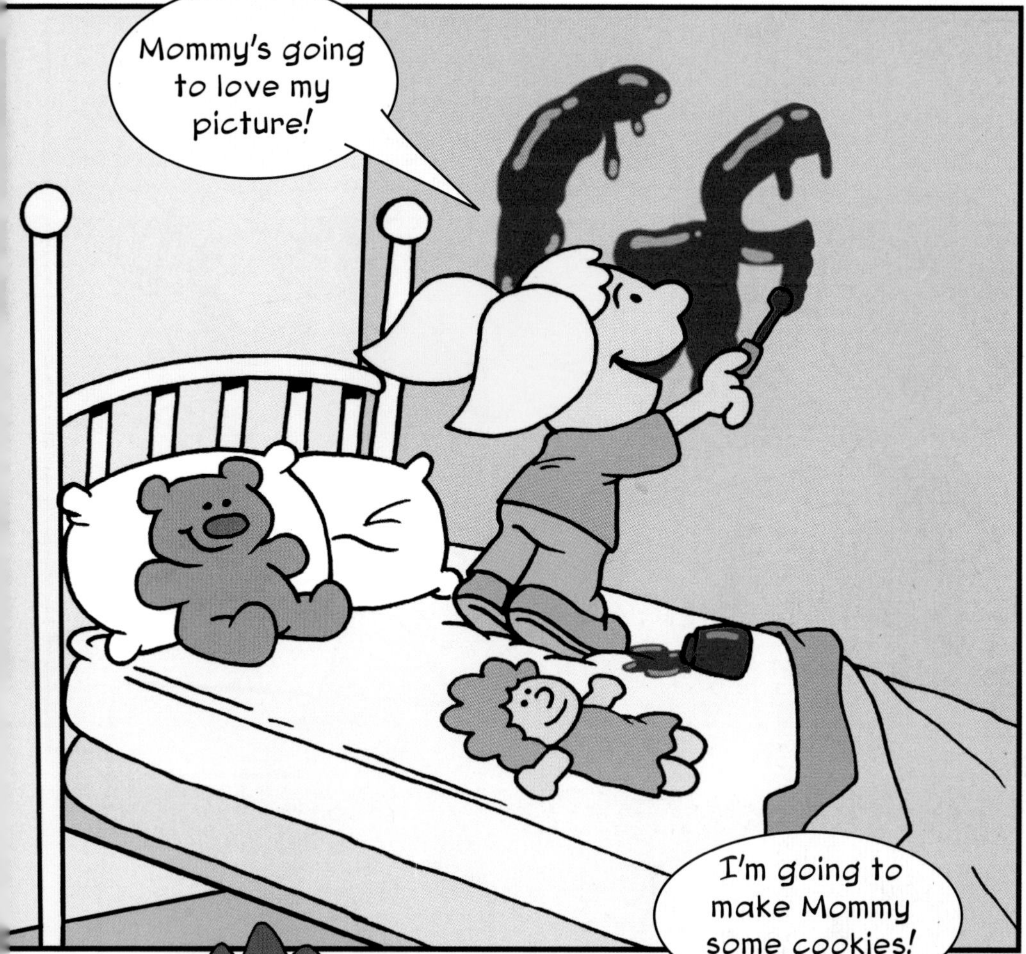
Mommy's going to love my picture!

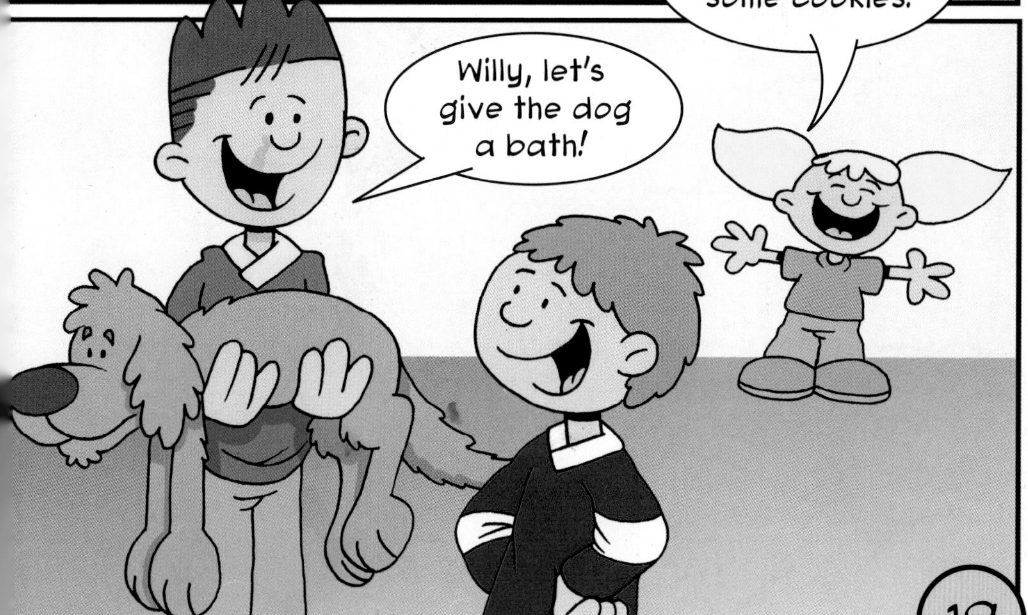
I'm going to make Mommy some cookies!
Willy, let's give the dog a bath!

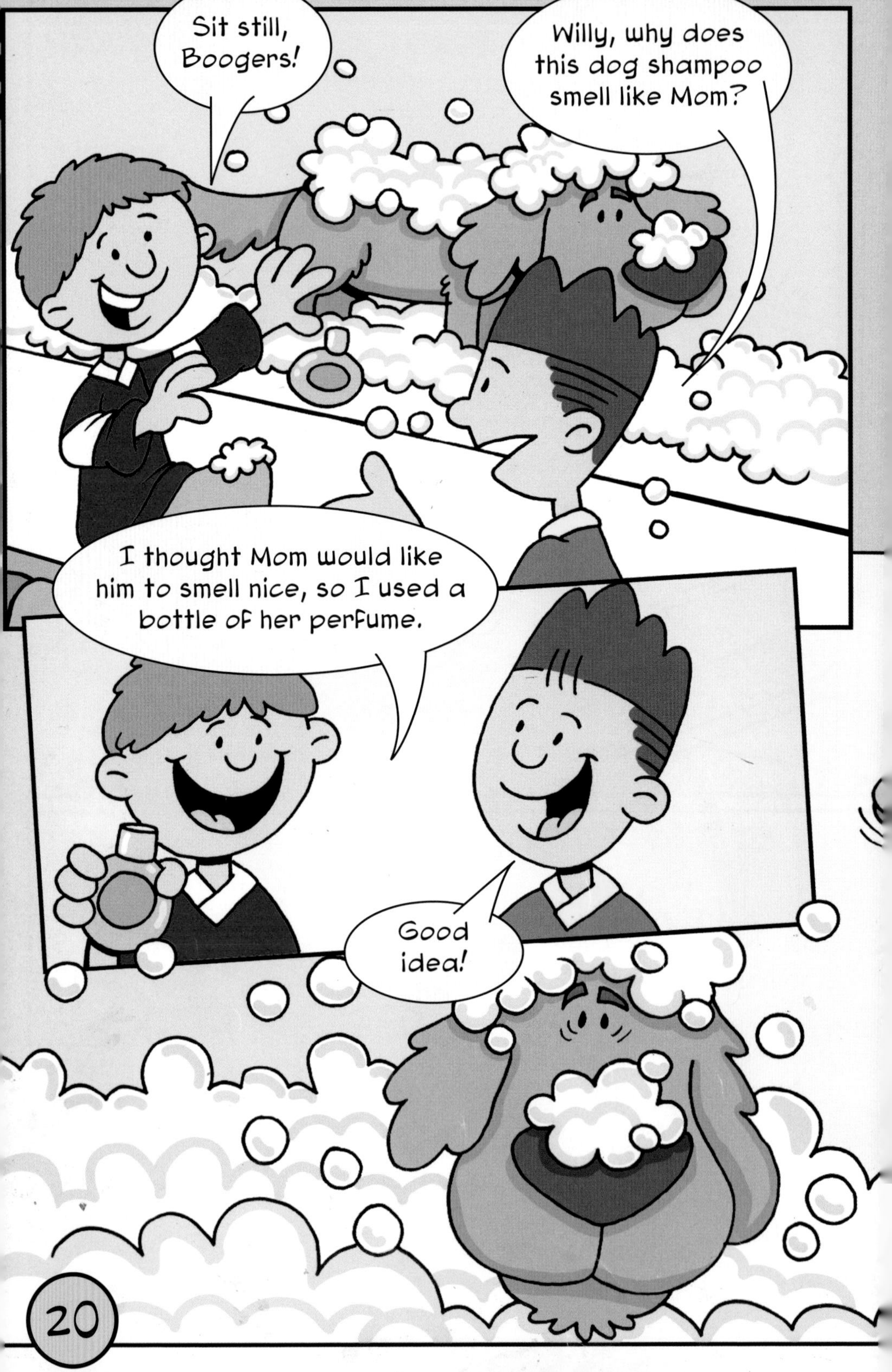
Sit still, Boogers!
Willy, why does this dog shampoo smell like Mom?
I thought Mom would like him to smell nice, so I used a bottle of her perfume.
Good idea!

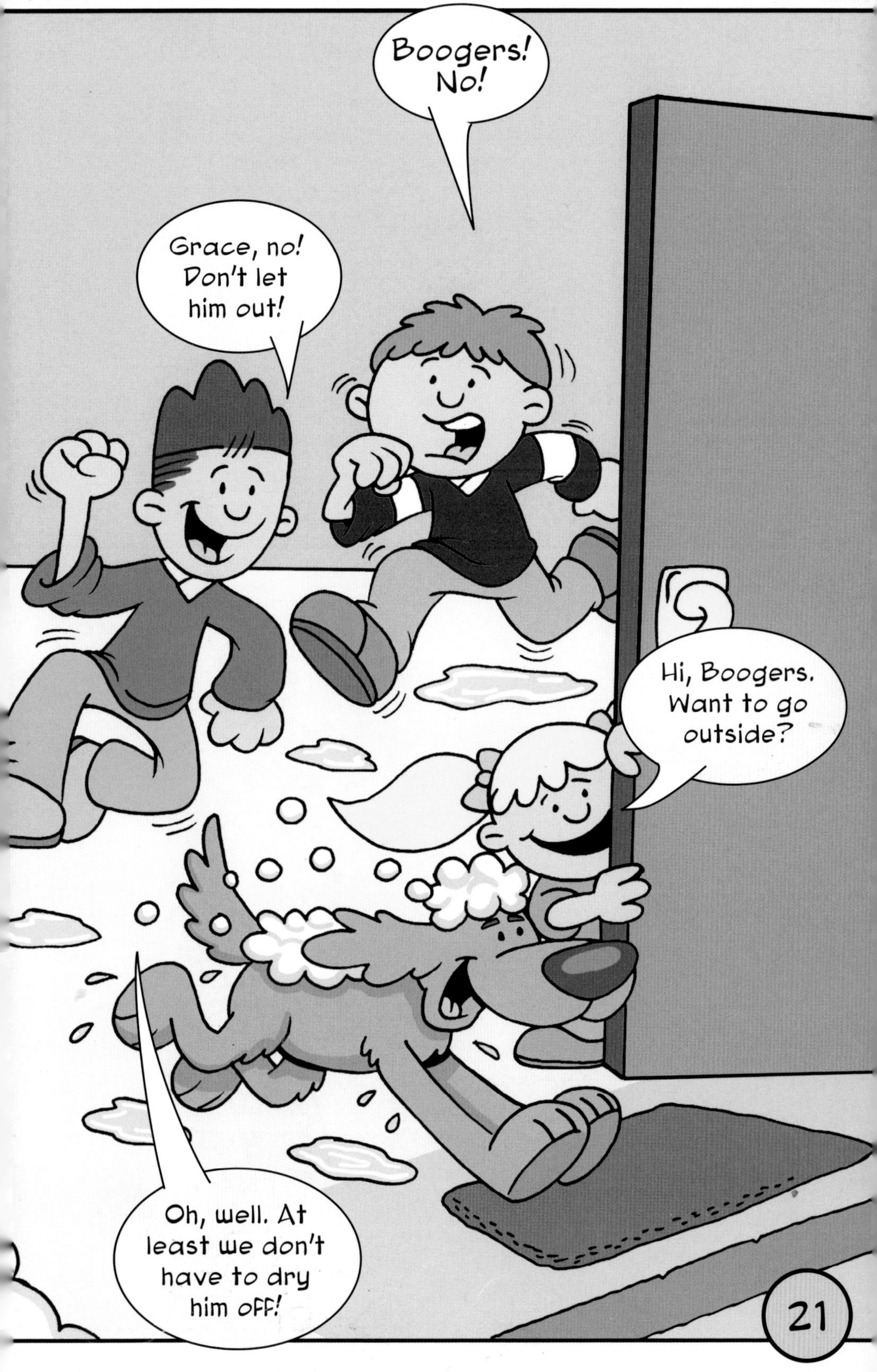
Boogers! No!
Grace, no! Don't let him out!
Hi, Boogers. Want to go outside?
Oh, well. At least we don't have to dry him off!

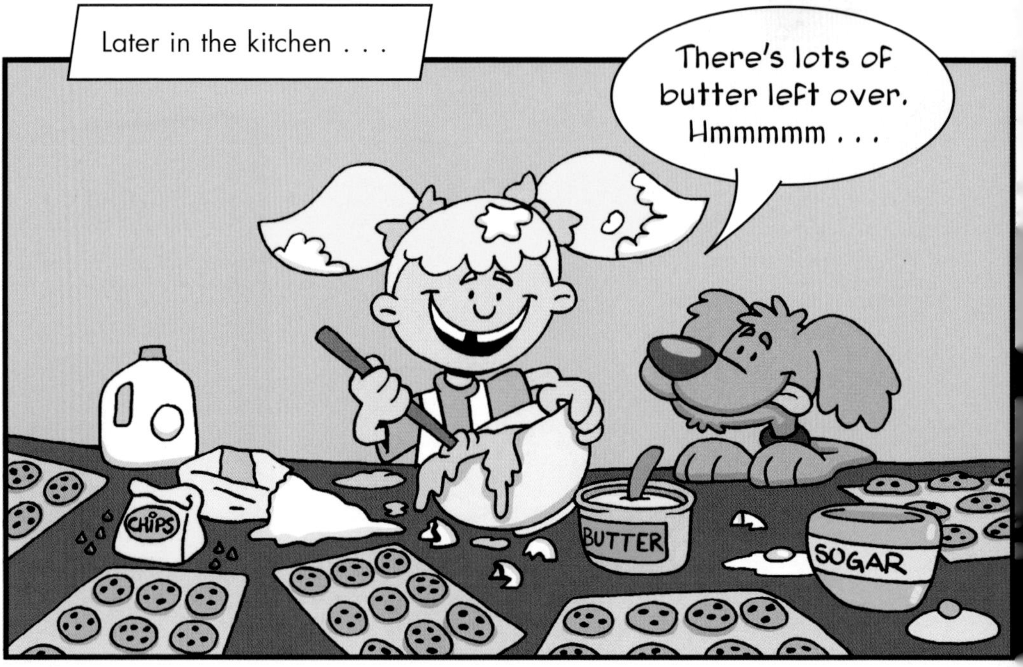
Later in the kitchen . . .
There's lots of butter left over. Hmmmmm . . .
CHIPS
BUTTER

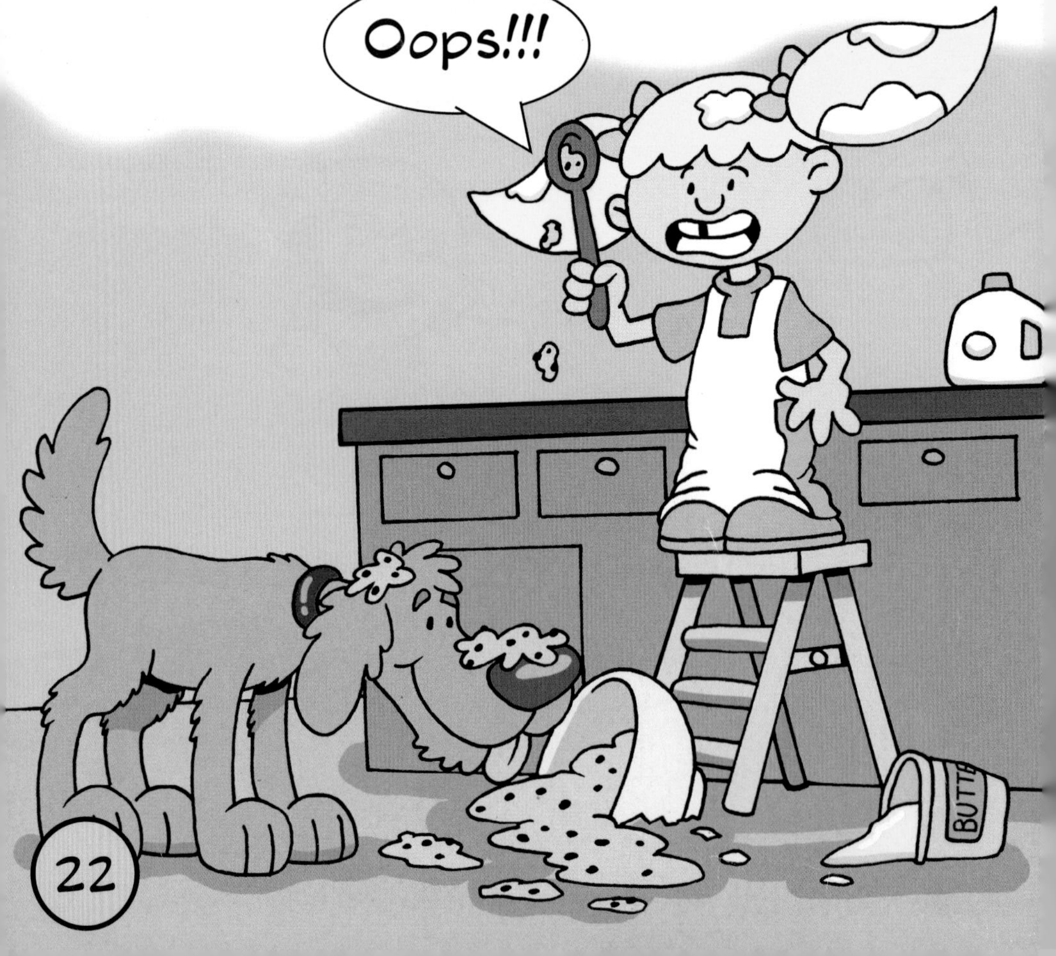
Oops!!!

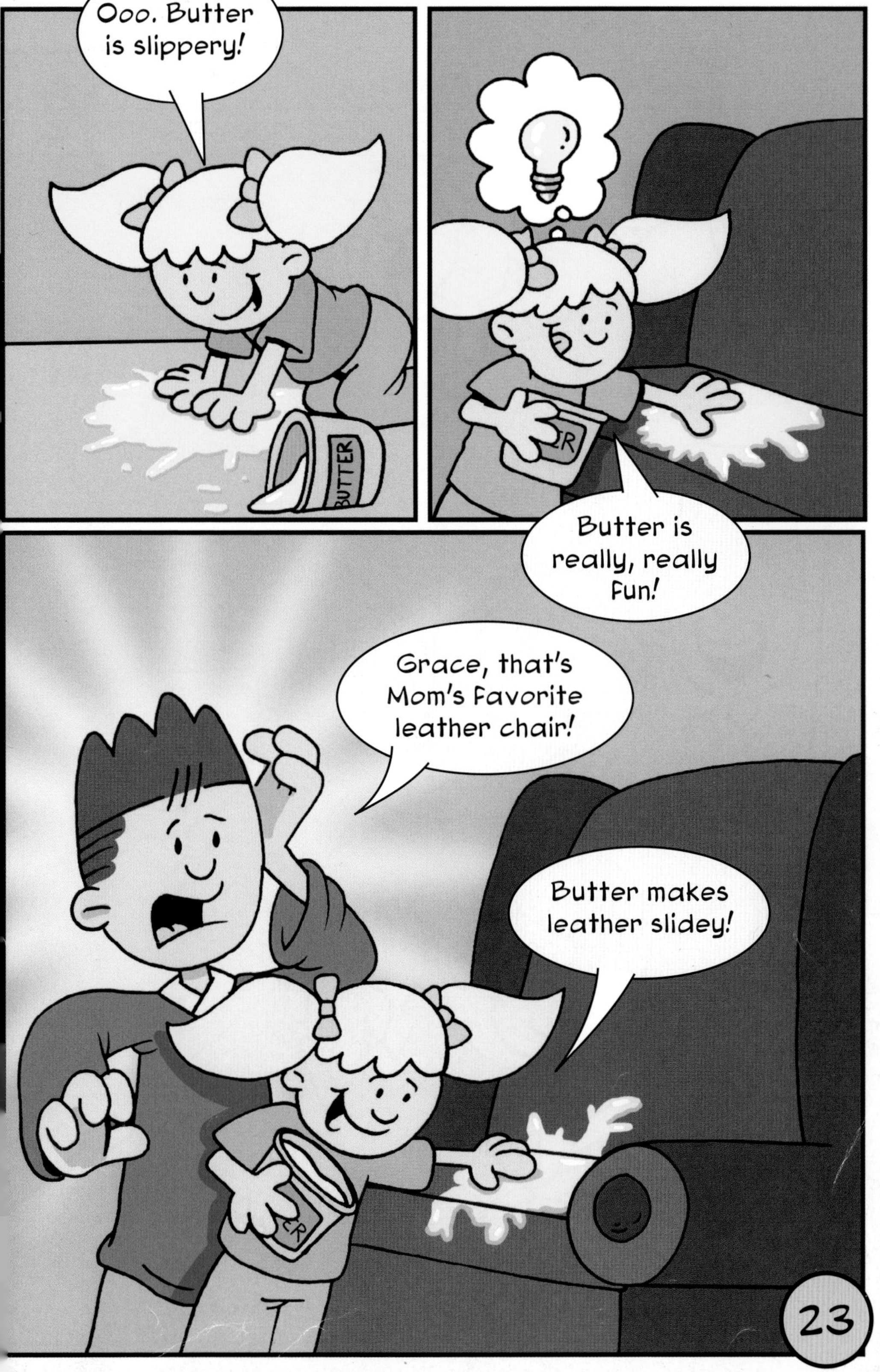
Ooo. Butter is slippery!
BUTTER
Butter is really, really fun!
Grace, that's Mom's favorite leather chair!
Butter makes leather slidey!

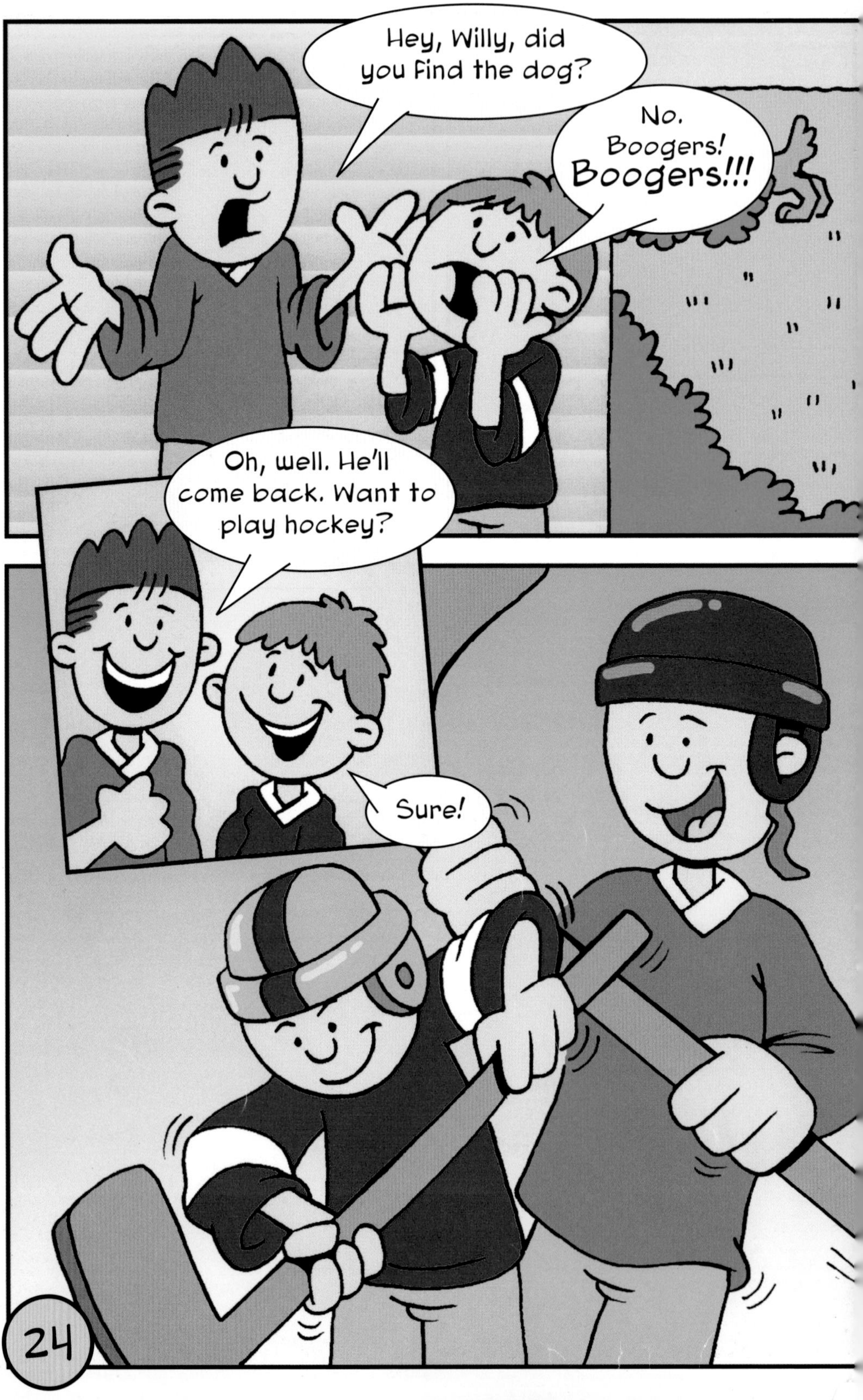
Hey, Willy, did you find the dog?
No. Boogers! Boogers!!!
Oh, well. He'll come back. Want to play hockey?
Sure!

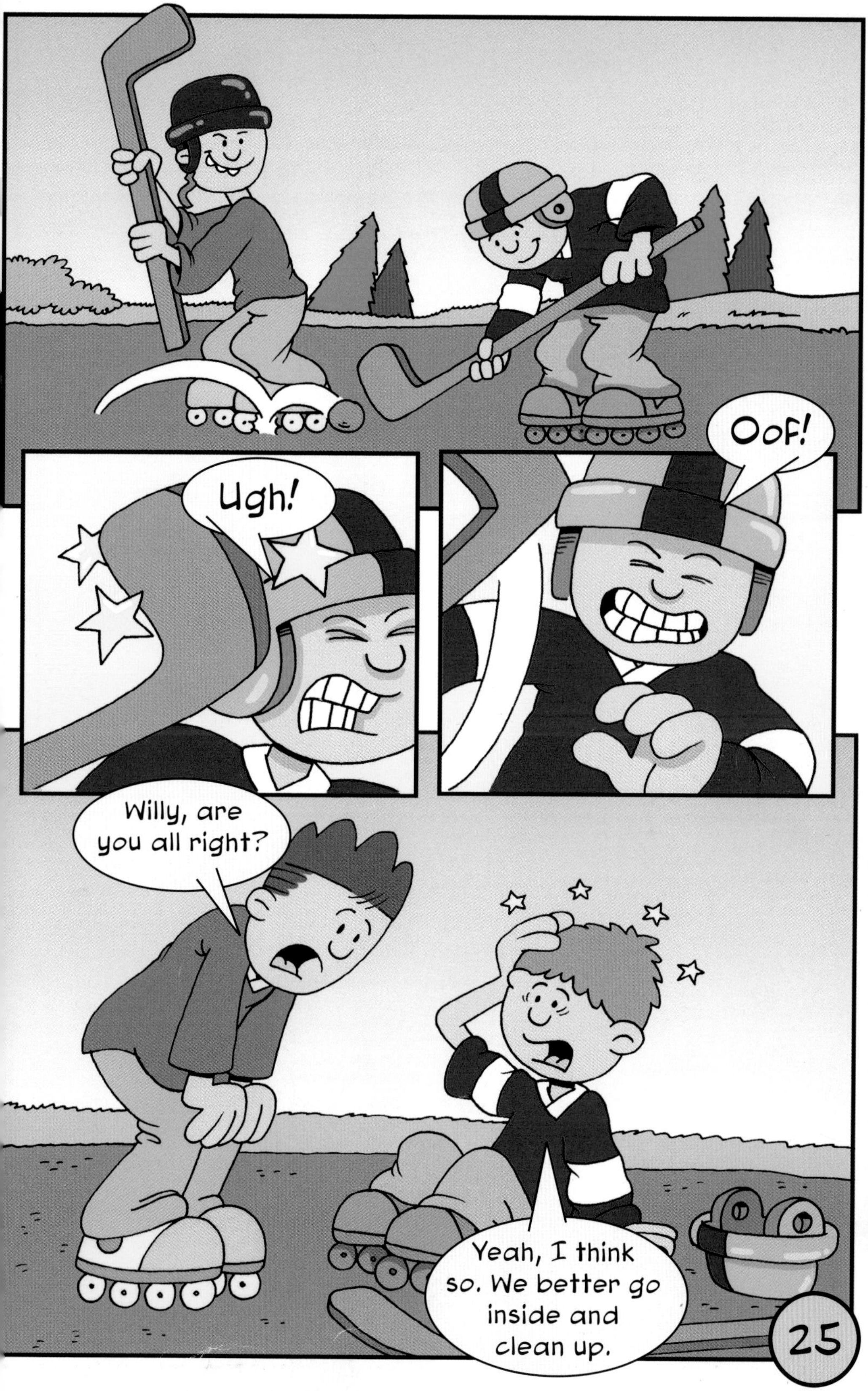
Oof!
Ugh!
Willy, are you all right?
Yeah, I think so. We better go inside and clean up.

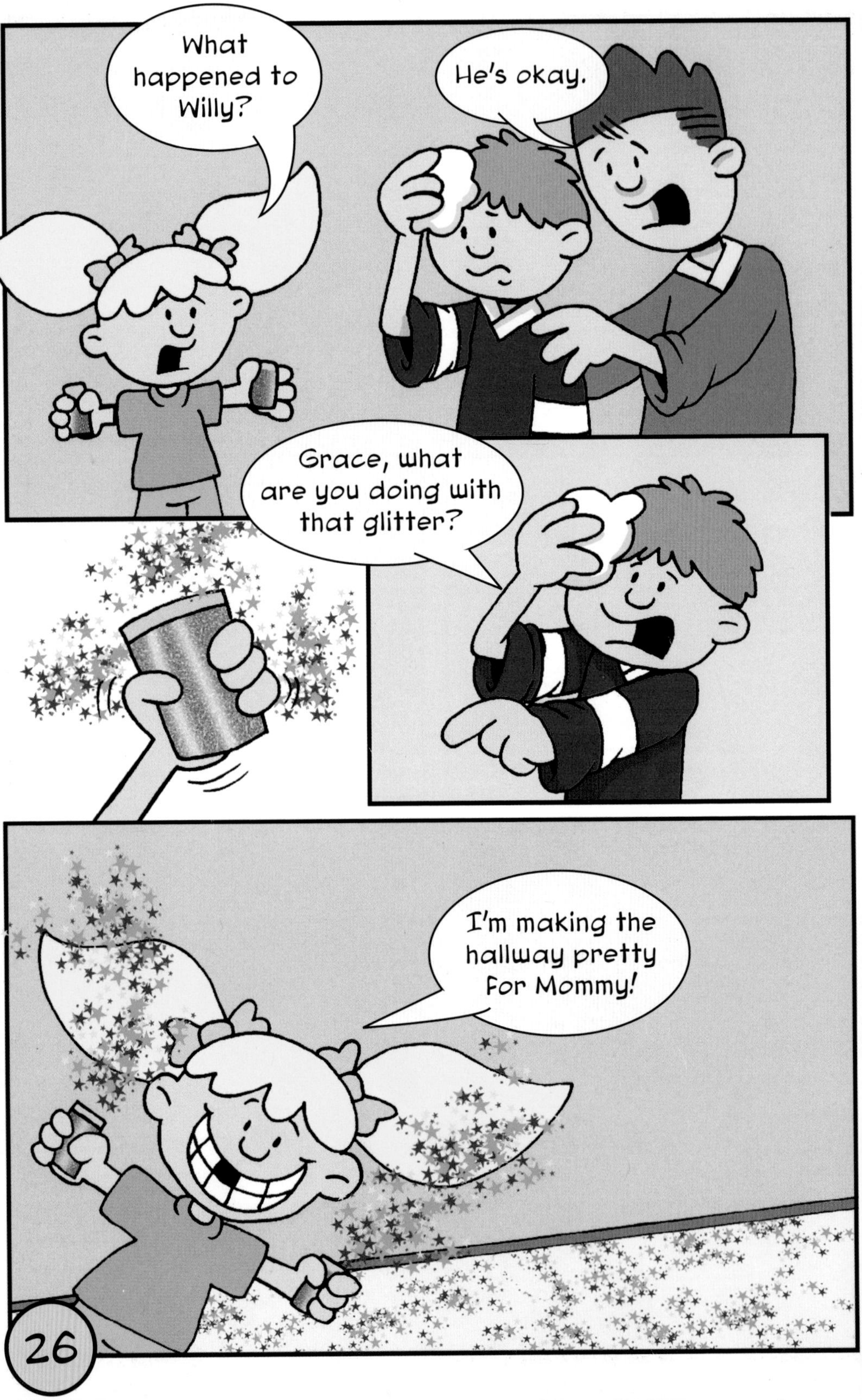
What happened to Willy?
He's okay.
Grace, what are you doing with that glitter?
I'm making the hallway pretty for Mommy!

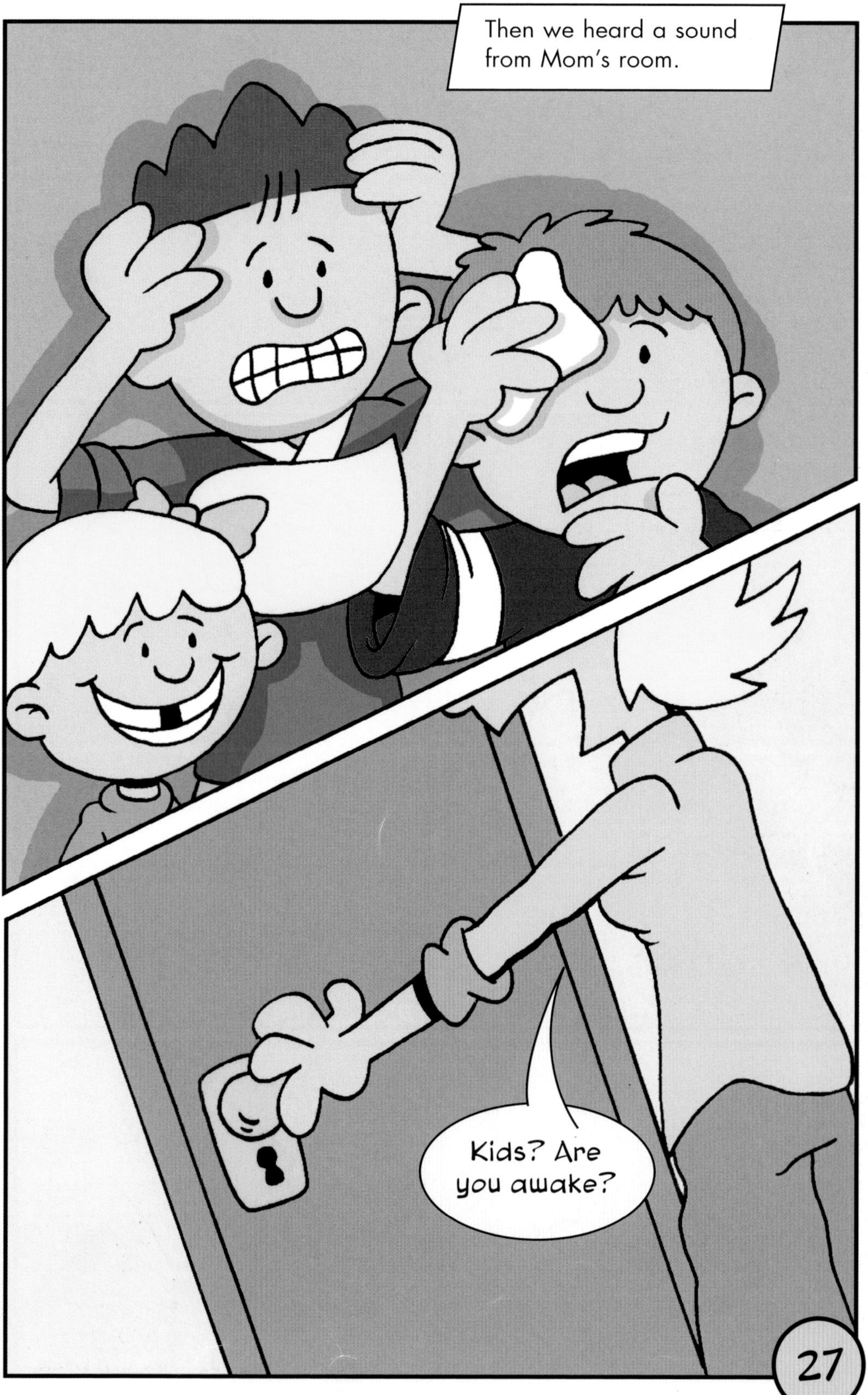
Then we heard a sound from Mom's room.
Kids? Are you awake?

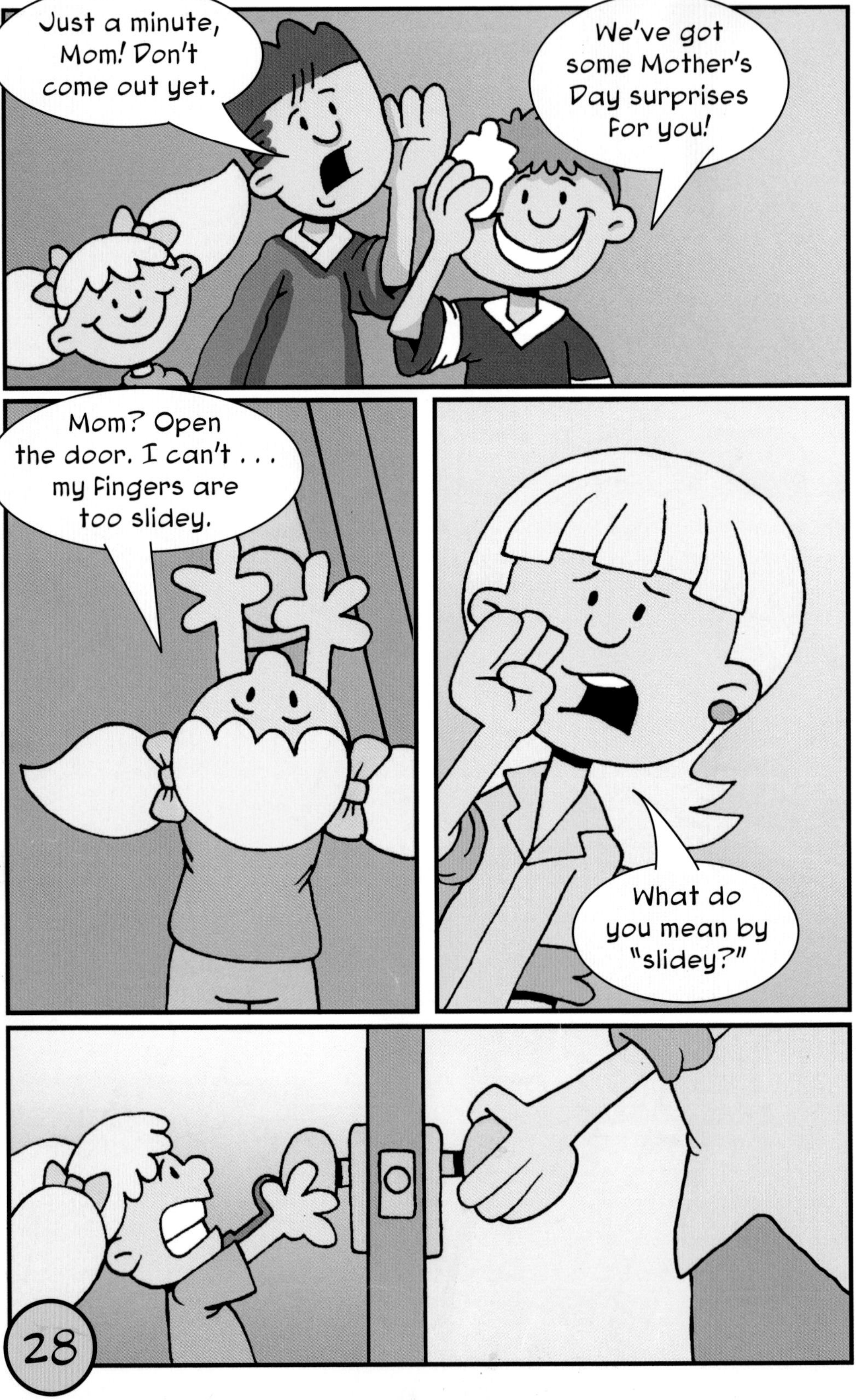
Just a minute, Mom! Don't come out yet.
We've got some Mother's Day surprises for you!
Mom? Open the door. I can't . . . my fingers are too slidey.
What do you mean by "slidey?"

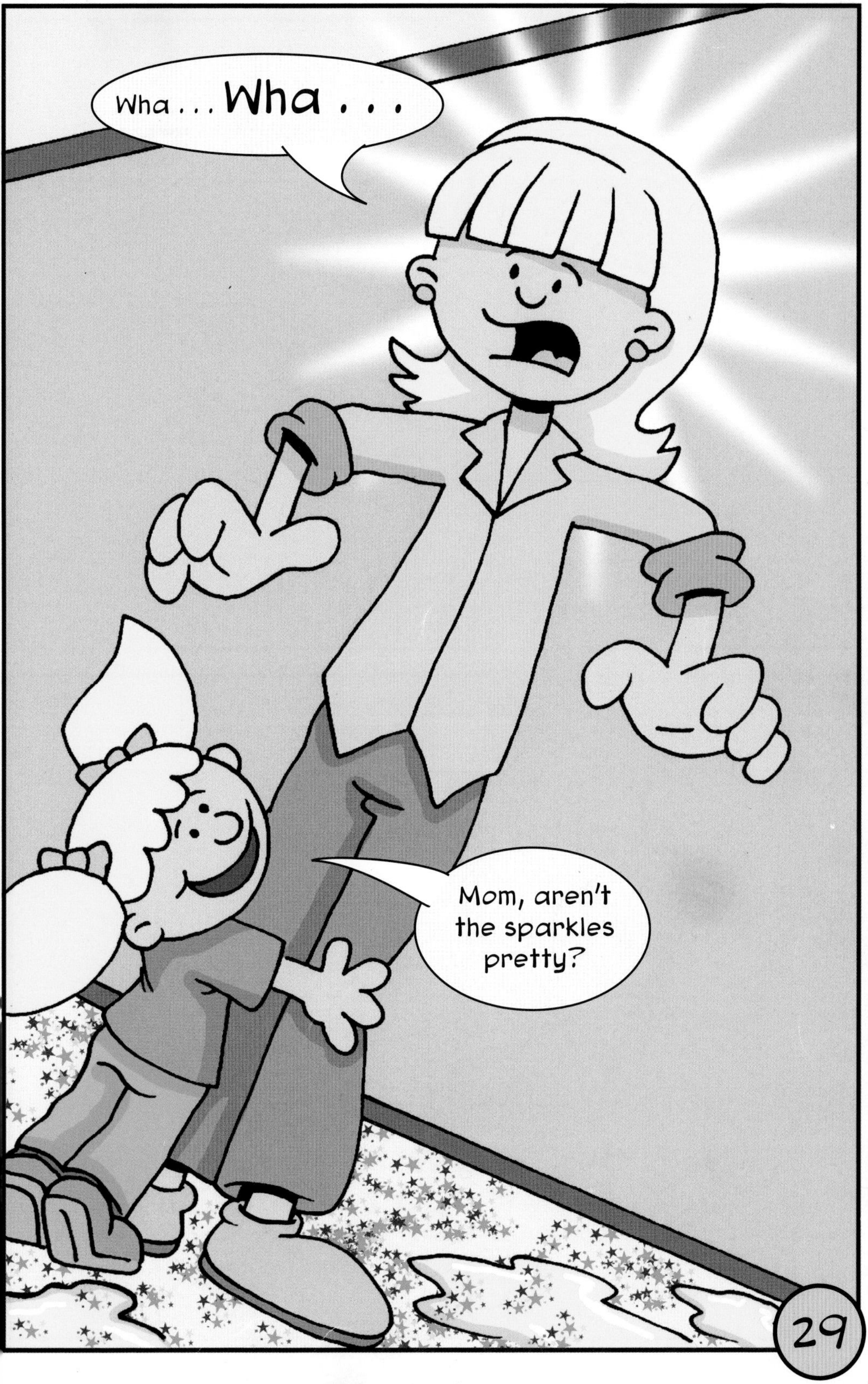
Wha . . . Wha . . .
Mom, aren't the sparkles pretty?

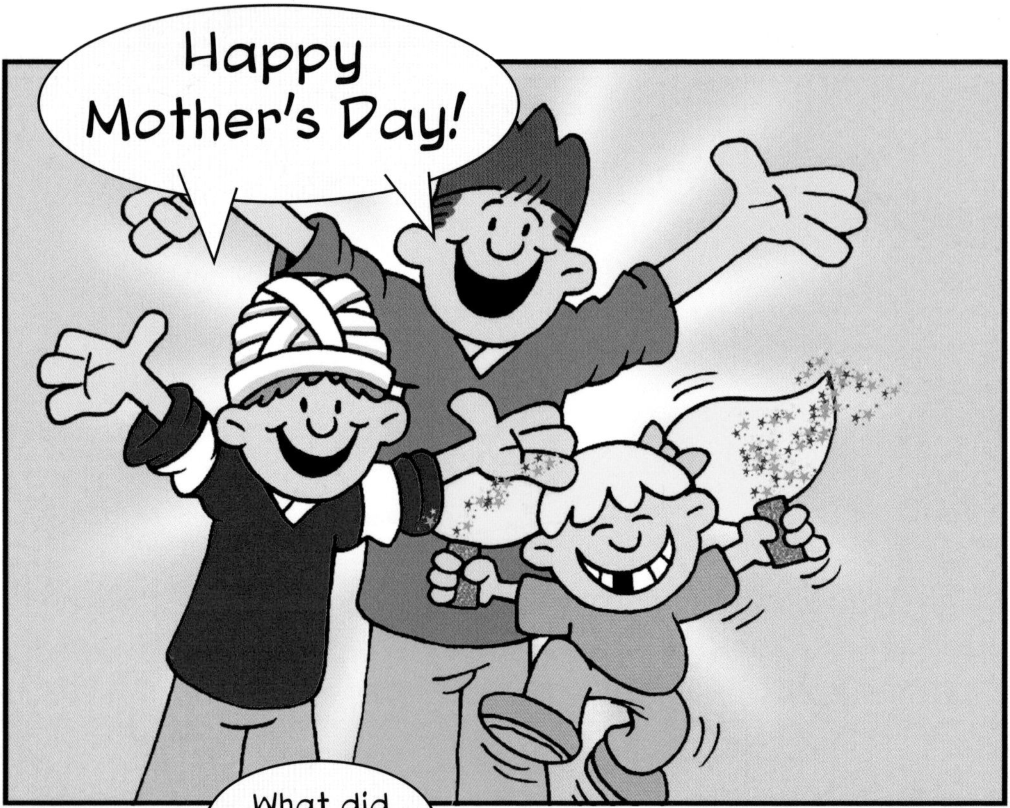
Happy Mother's Day!

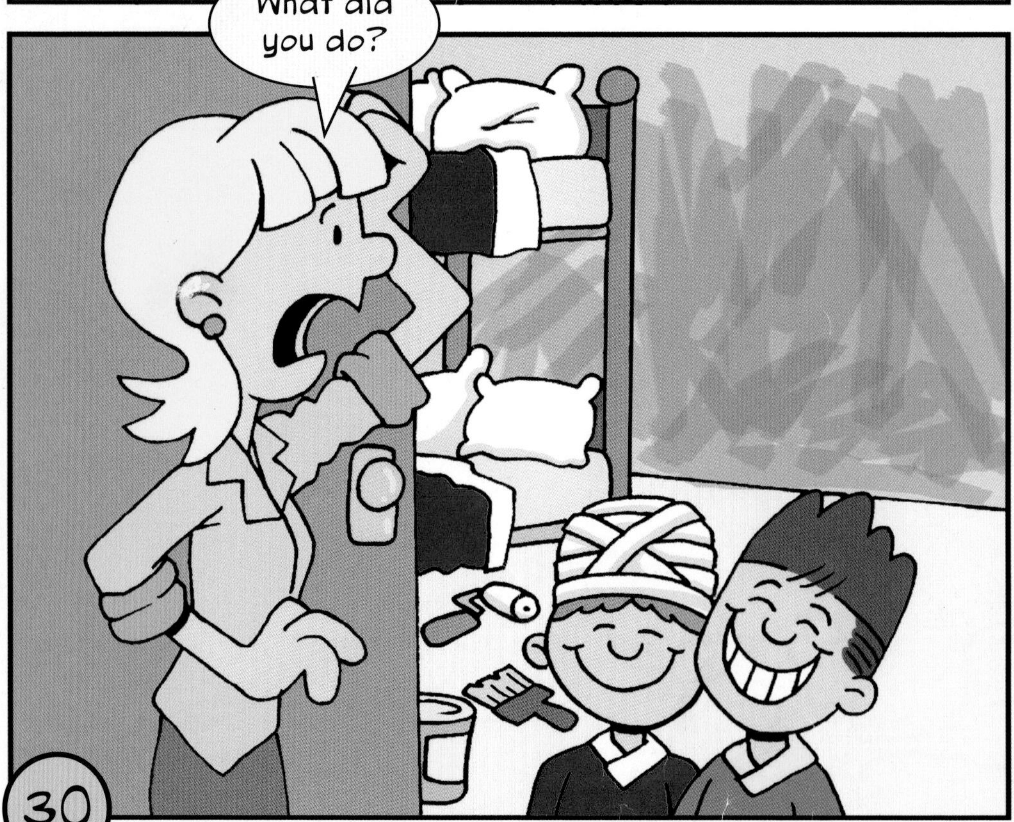
What did you do?

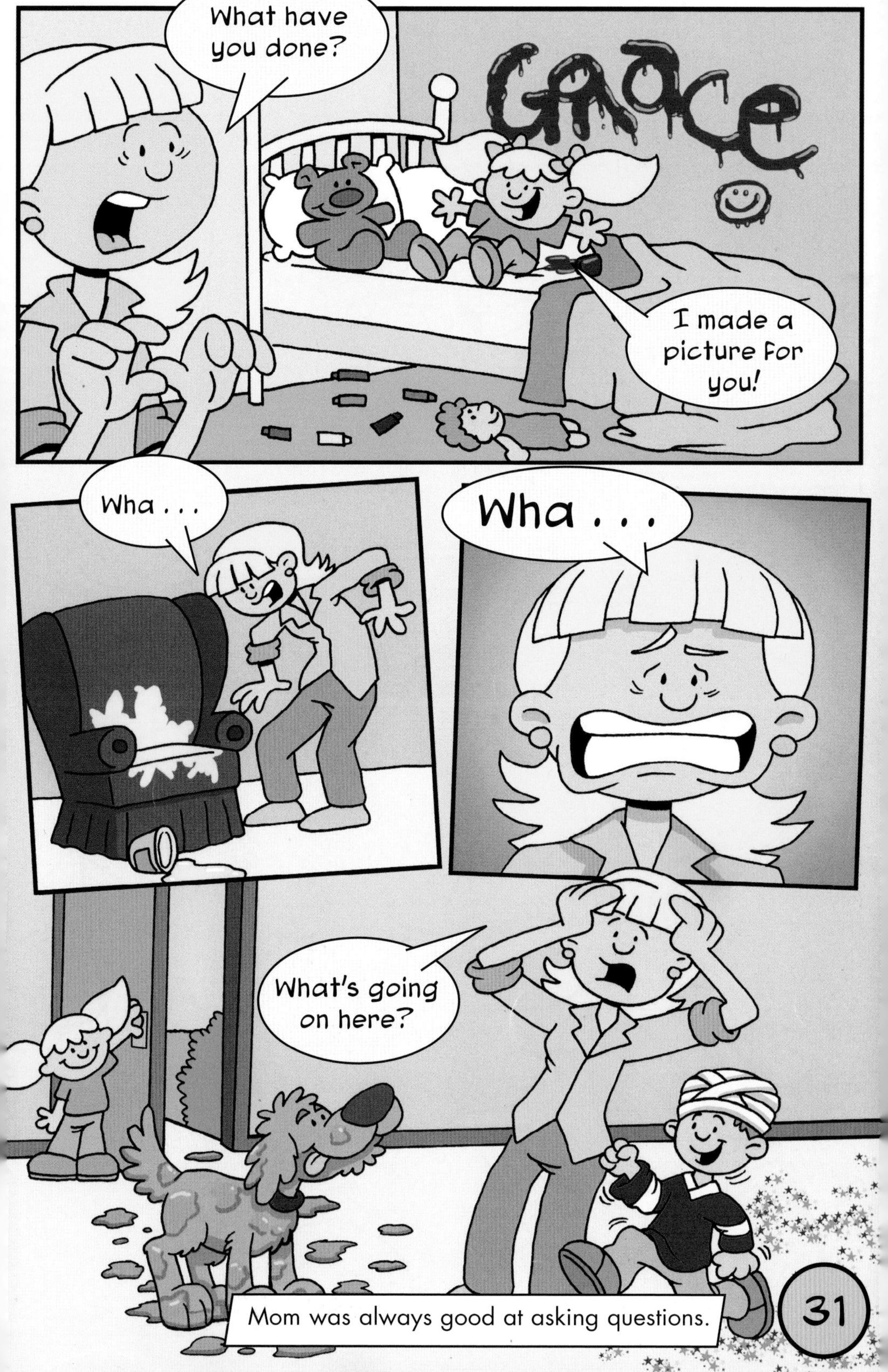
What have you done?
GRACE
I made a picture for you!
Wha . . .
Wha . . .
What's going on here?

Mom was always good at asking questions.

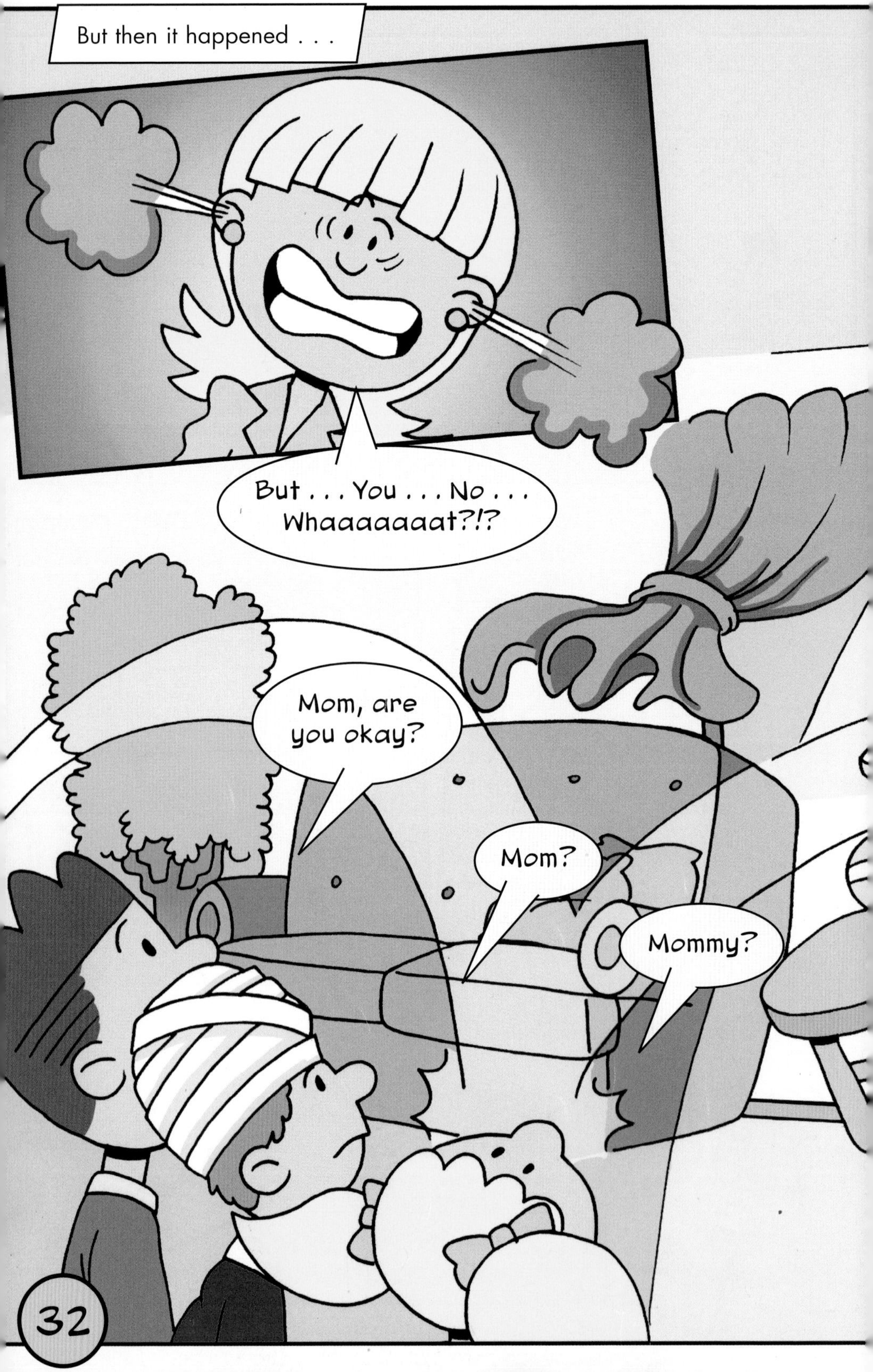
But then it happened . . .
But . . . You . . . No . . . Whaaaaaaat?!?
Mom, are you okay?
Mom?
Mommy?

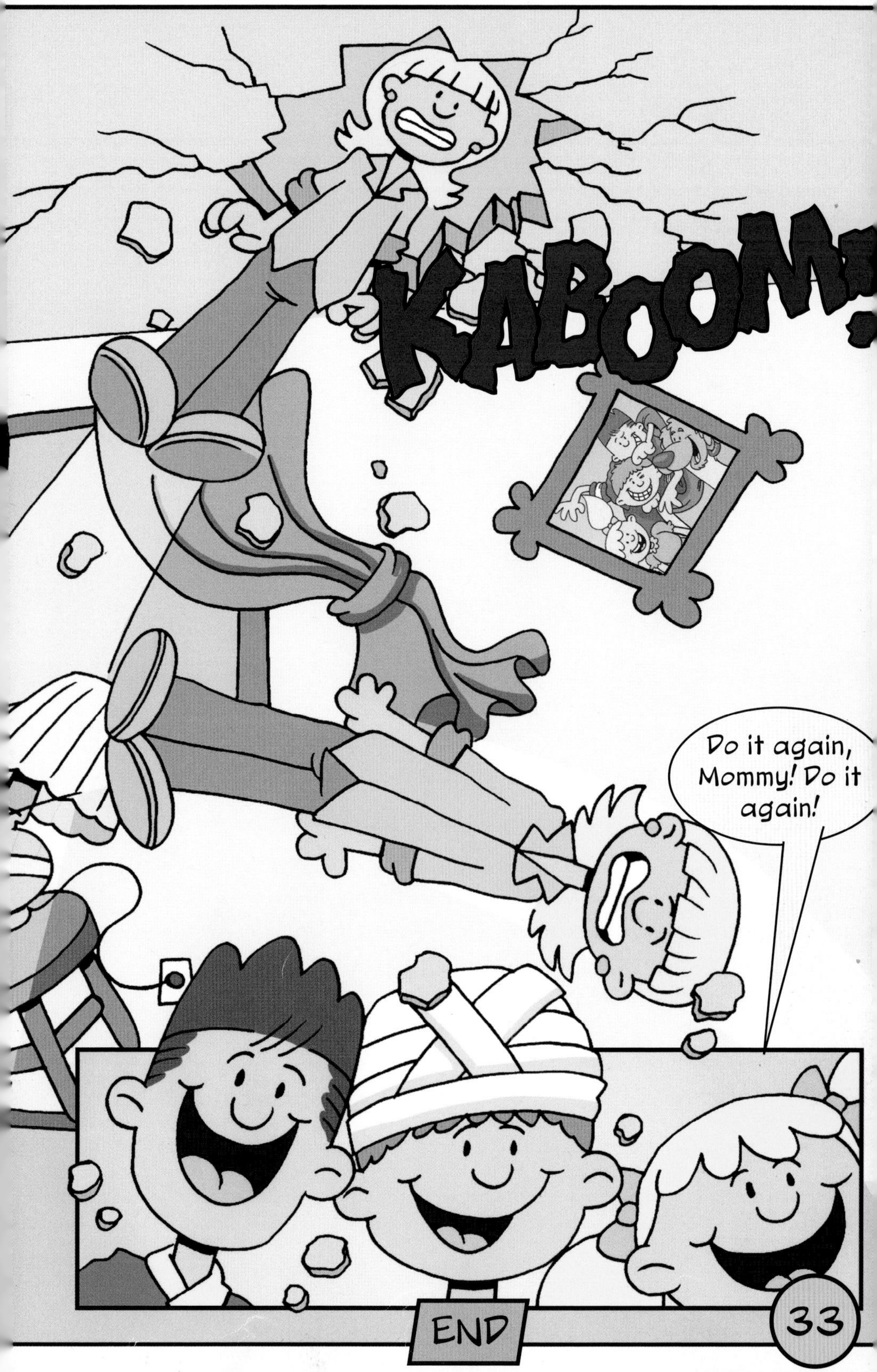
KABOOM!
Do it again, Mommy! Do it again!
END

ABOUT THE AUTHOR

Bob Temple has three children of his own, and he knows what it feels like when things get a little crazy at home. In fact, some of the things in this book are things that have actually happened in Bob's family! Bob has written more than 30 books for children.

ABOUT THE ILLUSTRATOR

Steve Harpster has loved to draw funny cartoons, mean monsters, and goofy gadgets since he was able to pick up a pencil. In first grade, he was able to avoid his writing assignments by working on the pictures for stories instead.

Steve was able to land a job drawing funny pictures for books, and that's really what he's best at. Steve lives in Columbus, Ohio, with his wonderful wife, Karen, and their sheepdog, Doodle.

GLOSSARY

boogers (BOO-gurz) stuff that comes out of your nose, also a cool name for a pet

handful (HAND-ful) a nice word a mother might use to describe her child; it really means "this kid drives me nuts!"

insane (in-SAYN) crazy or wacko

paint thinner (PAYNT THIN-ur) a liquid that is added to paint to make it thinner

project (PROJ-ekt) a special plan or idea. Try using this word to sound more important. When your mother asks, "What are you doing in your room?" instead of saying, "We're making a mess," say, "We're working on a project."

slidey (SLY-dee) a made-up word that means slippery

snap (SNAP) to lose control, get crazy, go nuts, blow up, explode, hit the roof; mothers often snap after their kids do special "projects."

THE SCOOP ON CHOCOLATE CHIPS

Chocolate chip cookies are also known as toll house cookies.

The first chocolate chip cookies were baked in the Toll House Restaurant of Massachusetts. The restaurant was built on the site of an old toll house, a place where travelers 200 years ago paid a toll, or fee, to use the road that ran past the house.

In 1937, Ruth and Kenneth Wakefield owned the Toll House Restaurant. Ruth made treats for her guests. One day Ruth ran out of powdered chocolate, so she took a bar of chocolate and cut it into chunks. She thought the chunks would dissolve into the rest of the cookie dough. Instead, the chunks only melted a little, making an amazing and delicious surprise. Chocolate chip cookies were made by accident!

Making cookies is a snap! Here's some cool stuff to chew on while you're cleaning up the kitchen.

Be careful eating chocolate near your pets. A chemical in chocolate can be poisonous to dogs. If your dog accidentally eats chocolate, feed it some burnt toast! Seriously. Then call a pet doctor.

People in the United States eat more chocolate than anywhere else.

A chocolate chip weighs 1/54 of an ounce. It weighs less than a housefly!

In France, "le chocolate" is slang for dog poop.

DISCUSSION QUESTIONS

1) Willy says his Mom calls him a "bundle of
   energy." She calls his brother "electric" and
   his little sister "a handful." What do you think
   his Mom really means?

2) Willy and Tom want to surprise their mom
   by painting their room all by themselves. Is
   that a good idea? What kind of surprise
   would be better?

3) What actually made Mom snap? Was she
   angry, or upset, or Feeling something else?

1.) Have you ever "snapped?" Write about what made you get that way.

2.) Have you ever done something special for someone on their birthday or a holiday? Write what you did and if you would do anything differently the next time.

3.) Think about what life would be like if you were a parent and had your own kids. Do you think they would ever make you "snap?" Write a story telling what your imaginary children did that made you "go crazy."

INTERNET

Do you want to know more about subjects related to this book? Or are you interested in learning about other topics? Then check out FactHound, a fun, easy way to find Internet sites.

Our investigative staff has already sniffed out great sites for you!

Here's how to use FactHound:

1.) Visit www.Facthound.com

2.) Select your grade level.

3.) To learn more about subjects related to this book, type in the book's ISBN number: **1598890387**. If you're looking for information on another subject, simply type in a keyword.

4.) Click the *Fetch It* button.

FactHound will fetch the best Internet sites for you.